EVERY F
TELLS A S   RY

Greg Moody

*For Damien, Alison and Megan, none of whom I've ever met,
but all of whom unwittingly inspired me to write this book.*

Spring 1981

Chapter 1

Flecks of saliva showered into the air as the dog barked at Spike, its head back and nose pointing at the sky. Every time it opened and closed its huge mouth, he got a brief glimpse of a formidable set of off-white teeth before the powerful jaws snapped shut and the sound from its vocal cords hit his eardrums.

It had run the length of the front garden of the house that he had been approaching, causing him to halt on the pavement beside the gate that he had been about to open. A low wall was all that separated him from the creature, which stared at him with menacingly dark eyes made more sinister by the furrows that ran above them across its brow. It was close enough for him to be able to smell its hot breath mixed with the canine odour lifting from its body. Judging by the dog's muscular frame, the wall looked unlikely to provide Spike with any kind of protection should it decide to do more than just frighten him away.

Between the bouts of barking came the unmistakable sound of another pair of claws scraping on a concrete path as a second large animal turned the corner of the house at speed and tried to gain traction. Spike looked up to see a dog of a similar powerful breed, but larger than the first and lighter-coloured, race around the side of the house into the front garden to join in the dispute, doubtless summoned by the first dog's alarm calls. Now there was double the anger, double the noise and double the threat.

Just as Spike was considering moving away, the front door opened with a loose rattling sound and a large man appeared on the doorstep. He was dressed in baggy tracksuit trousers, dirty plimsolls and a thin white vest. His arms appeared to be purple, such was the proliferation of tattoos covering them, beneath the multitude of forearm hair, along with much of his torso and neck, the dark pattern working its way up one side of his shaven head.

He yelled something unintelligible at the dogs, but with sufficient menace in his voice to bring a temporary halt to the constant barking, before turning his attention to Spike. He folded his arms, the muscles standing out beneath the coating of hair.

"Whatever you're selling, we don't want none!" he declared, with the finality of someone not used to being contradicted.

"I live just around the corner," said Spike, gesturing in the direction that he had come from. "I thought you'd like to know that there's a reporter bloke knocking on front doors, asking about the chap with the dangerous dogs."

The man on the doorstep shifted his stance slightly on hearing a reply that he hadn't been expecting. Spike took advantage of the lull to expand on his message.

"He said something about a court order to have them confiscated, on account of an incident in the park, and he wanted to know what we thought, as your neighbours."

The man made his way down the path, calling his dogs to him and taking hold of the chunky metal collars around their substantial necks. The opportunity for closer inspection of the man showed Spike that he had a gold earring and a nose piercing, and even the palms of his hands had been tattooed.

"He can go and get stuffed!" the man told his visitor. "They can all get stuffed! If they want a fight, I'll give 'em one. They'll 'ave to shoot me first and carry me out in a body bag before they can get their hands on 'em, and that's a promise. I'll take the lot of 'em to court and win, 'cos I've got right on my side. No one tells me what to do. I do what I like. So, they can bring it on, 'cos they'll only end up losers. My boys aren't going nowhere."

"Have you had them long?" asked Spike as the man's anger eased.

"I've known 'em since they was puppies. Them's bruvvers. They was bred by a mate of mine, but he had domestic trouble, so I said I'd look after them." He cupped the head of the larger one in front of his own, addressing him personally, but the dog didn't seem impressed and jerked its head free.

"What breed are they?"

The man straightened upright, back on eye level with Spike. "They'm Japanese fighting dogs, but you don't want to believe what you hear. They got a lovely nature with those that they know. They're great with the kids. My mate's nipper rides on the back of him and he don't so much as growl. People is quick to judge. They take one look and say they'm dangerous, but if you come round my house of an evening you'd see 'em stretched out by the fire and you'd wonder what all the fuss were about.

"It's all a put-up job, anyhow. If that kid hadn't tormented 'em, nuffink would have happened. They'm as good as gold when they're wiv me. And that other kid was eating summat and they was hungry. If they'd left him alone, nuffink would 'ave 'appened. But people don't want to hear about that. They makes their minds up wivout knowing the facts and think there's only one answer."

He looked closely at Spike. "Where d'you say you live?"

Spike started to point up the road, past the line of hedges, but then stopped in mid-sentence. "Hang on. That bloke who knocked on my door is coming down this way."

The man with the tattoos pulled his dogs back up the path towards his house, holding on to the collars, throwing a quick: "I owe you one," over his shoulder as he hustled them inside and shut the door.

Spike walked on along the pavement and around the corner to where he had parked his old Austin Allegro, and got into the driver's seat. Before starting the engine, he reached into his top pocket and lifted out a small tape machine. It whirred as he pressed the rewind button and then a voice sounded from the speaker when he pressed 'Play'.

"They'll 'ave to shoot me first and carry me out in a body bag before they can get their hands on 'em, and that's a promise." He smiled to himself and pocketed the machine. "I do love it when a plan comes together."

The stone steps that led to the front entrance of the *Bartown Chronicle* had been worn to a dip in the middle with the countless feet that had made their way up them over the nearly one hundred years since it was launched. The smooth downward curves always seemed welcoming to Spike, a reassuring presence, like a favourite armchair that fits your frame, providing a familiar feeling underfoot when he returned with a story to be written.

The steps matched the newspaper's offices and indeed much of the town in that they were as worn and comfortable as an old slipper. The majority of the population of Bartown were of pension age, comfortably retired and resistant to change, and though there were dusty corners and you could spot peeling paintwork in places on the old buildings if you looked closely enough, most of the people liked it that way and felt reassured by the adherence to old ways.

The two ladies who ran the front office were a formidable duo. Their long service lent them an air of authority borne of knowing how everything needed to be done, and they dealt with callers who placed adverts or bought a paper with a firmness that stopped just short of brusqueness.

They were kept busy by the steady flow of customers, leaving little time to gossip with those that they knew who had come up to town to do some shopping. Even during quiet spells, the phone would ring, keeping them fully occupied, or a member of staff would appear from the offices through the connecting door behind them to request a form for expenses or drop an envelope in the tray to be collected by the postman.

Spike offered them a brief hello as he made his way around the counter and on through the swing door that led to the reporters' room behind, where his desk was arranged sideways to the far wall. Most of the surface of it was covered by a big, black Imperial manual typewriter, and what little room was left held a large grey telephone and a pile of carbon copies of stories that he had written, impaled on a six-inch metal rod pointing towards the ceiling from its round base of wood, known as a 'spike'.

In his early days in the profession, he had pondered whether, given his nickname, he had always been destined to follow the journalistic calling, in the way that people working in the clothing business are often called Taylor, or roofing contractors have the surname Thatcher. Some things were meant to be, and who was he to argue?

The room was empty of any of his colleagues, so Spike began writing his story, playing back the quotes on his portable tape machine and hammering the keys of his typewriter as the tale unfolded. The noise was punctuated by the 'ding' of the margin bell that signaled the end of each line and the need to swipe the carriage return lever to take the paper down to the next space on the sheet.

When he had amassed half a dozen hand-size pages, torn from the double-ply roll that was fed through his typewriter from the back, he read through them, correcting some misspellings and typing errors until he was satisfied.

He dialed a number on the phone that he had scribbled on a piece of paper pinned to the wall next to his desk, connecting him with the *Chronicle*'s sister daily paper ten miles away, and waited for the woman's voice to answer. "Copy desk, please," he told her, and soon another woman's voice came through the phone. "Story for the *Evening Post*," he said. "Catchline: dogs. Byline: Stephen Pike." He started the dictation:

"A dog owner who faces jail for having two dangerously out-of-control pets has vowed to die rather than have them confiscated. Darren Rumsey intends to fight efforts to part him with his two Japanese fighting dogs, saying: 'My boys aren't going nowhere. They'll 'ave to shoot me first and carry me out in a body bag before they can get their hands on 'em, and that's a promise.'

"Unemployed Mr Rumsey, of Hitchcock Avenue, Bartown, is being investigated by police following an incident in nearby Greenacres Park, in which two children needed hospital treatment after allegedly being bitten by his dogs.

"He claims that the two male animals, which he has known since they were puppies, were not to blame for the attack, suggesting that the children were tormenting his pets, and the incident occurred because one of the youngsters was eating.

"'It's all a put-up job, anyhow,' he claimed. 'If that kid in the play area hadn't tormented them, nothing would have happened. They're as good as gold when they're with me.

"'They can all get stuffed! If they want a fight, I'll give them one. I'll take the lot of them to court and win, because I've got right on my side.'

"But local people have expressed fears about living near to the animals. One neighbour, who didn't want to be named, said: 'I won't walk past his house anymore. I go the long way round to the shops to avoid it, because he has them running round loose in his front garden barking at anyone who comes past. I just knew someone was going to get bitten sooner or later, and now it's happened to a couple of kids just playing in the park.'

"A police spokesman said: 'We are investigating a report of an incident involving two dogs in Greenacres Park at the weekend. A man in his forties has been interviewed by police, but a decision on whether to bring charges against him has yet to be made.

"'Two boys, aged seven and eight, were treated at Bartown General Hospital for minor injuries following the incident and have subsequently been released.'"

As he signed off with the copytaker and put the phone down, Spike looked up to see one of his colleagues had returned to the office, draping his heavy coat over the far side of his desk, which was next to the room's gas fire, in front of which he was now warming himself, rubbing his hands together briskly.

—

4

"Just been to see a man about a dog, have you?" quipped Carl. "Still got all your fingers?"

"He was quite chatty," Spike told him. "Even said he owed me a favour for helping him. Maybe I've made a new friend."

"Everyone has some good in them. As the ancient Chinese proverb says: 'Even the man who owns two dangerous dogs has to keep them well fed.'"

A whistle sounded from outside the room signaling that the kettle was boiling, and soon Carl returned with two mugs of coffee, made using a jar that they kept by the sink. Spike noticed that Carl had left his customary half inch gap at the top below the normally accepted level for a hot drink. A half bottle of whisky was slid out of Carl's pocket and used to make up the shortfall in both.

"A Mickey Finn, to keep out the cold," said Carl, returning to his place by the fire and taking a restorative gulp.

"What have you been up to?" asked Spike, more to show gratitude for the hot drink than because he wanted to know.

"Town council meeting," Carl replied, lighting a cigarette.

"Anything interesting?"

"Just the usual bickering about nothing of any importance. They are thinking of putting up some 'old people crossing' warning signs in the town, to get car drivers to slow down, with a silhouette of a bent-over couple with walking sticks in a red triangle. But they couldn't decide where they should put them, and after half an hour of arguing the toss, one of the councillors suggested they just have one at one end of the town and another at the other end, on account of its almost entirely geriatric population."

Carl took another grateful swig of his coffee. "It is getting like an old-people's home, this place." He made an expansive sweep of his arm, for theatrical effect. "They came to Bartown to die... and lived on... and on! Must be something in the water."

Just then the door opened and a third member of the reporting staff appeared. As editor, it was Tom's job to marshal his two newshounds into a productive unit of creative output, seeking items worthy of the printed page and turning them into stories.

"How were the Hounds of the Baskervilles?" asked Tom, pausing on his way to his office in the adjoining room.

"Loud and menacing, but their master spilled the beans. I've put the story over to the *Evening Post*, to keep them happy."

"Good. We need to keep them off our backs with a few of our more dramatic stories. There are rumblings about them sending a reporter over to be based here to keep them supplied with news. Anything we can do to make them think it's not needed would be welcome."

He turned to Carl. "I take it the council meeting didn't yield anything earth shattering enough to be fed their way?"

"Not unless a new set of salt bins for gritting the back road is likely to get their readers' pulses racing."

"Knock it out for our pages, and Spike have a mosey around town and see if you can sniff out a couple of stories, maybe even a feature. Ask around in the shops if there's anything interesting going on. Like I always say, if you turn over enough stones, you always find something hiding underneath one of them."

Chapter 2

The sun had come out as Spike emerged from the office, turning what had been a grey and gloomy day into one that seemed to offer more promise. Whenever he set out without a clear plan of where he was going and to whom he would be talking, but just on the hunt for something newsworthy, it was always with a sense of misgiving. He had heard tales from those in the industry who had done weekend shifts down in London of a national newspaper where there was a sign over the door as you were leaving saying: 'Don't come back without a story.'

It wasn't quite like that in a backwater like Bartown. If London was, by all accounts, the city that never sleeps, Bartown was the one that never wakes up. But still there was a feeling that to come back empty-handed would be a recognition of failure, and he took enough pride in his work never to want that to happen.

The guy in the garage would be a good place to start. He knew him from taking his car there, and so the ice would be broken without the need for an introduction.

Spike found him changing a tyre on a car at the front of the workshop, and leaned against the frame of the entrance, watching him expertly peeling the rubber from the metal wheel to look for the source of a puncture on the inner tube.

"Can't help you, I'm afraid," the man told him. "All quiet at this end. Plenty of customers, most of them wanting their cars mended but not wanting to wait, and then not wanting to pay for it when they're ready."

"What do you tell them?" asked Spike, who recalled having once overheard a fraught conversation when collecting his car involving a disappointed customer who had been told that he would have to wait until the following day for it to be finished.

"I point towards that sign," said the man, lifting his head up momentarily towards a wooden plaque on the wall. It read: 'Miracles we can manage; the impossible may take a little longer.'

Spike smiled. "I'd better leave you to it. I wouldn't want to be the cause of someone having to walk home tonight. I'll see you later."

There was a queue of customers just inside the entrance at the greengrocers, so Spike waited for it to shorten before going inside.

He asked for some apples, and as the shop owner was weighing them and pouring them into a brown paper bag, he explained his other reason for calling, and enquired whether anything of interest was going on.

"Next door's dog has just had a litter of puppies," he offered.

Spike pulled a face. "I think I've had enough of dogs for one day." He polished an apple on his jumper and took a bite.

"I need a new sign for over the shop door," said the man, brightening and warming to his theme. "The old one is looking a bit tatty. I thought I might change the name. The wife likes 'Grape Expectations', but I prefer 'Banana Republic'. What d'you think?"

Spike rolled his eyes and pocketed his bag of apples, turning for the door. "I'll let you know."

As he passed the newsagent's he noticed a display of 'For sale' cards in the window, placed by customers wanting to offload surplus items. As he munched his apple he scanned the adverts, offering pushchairs and kids' bikes, fridges and car roof-racks. One was rather different from the others. It was a printed card on a coloured background, unlike the simple notes scribbled in big letters in the hope of a quick sale. It read: 'Psychic Healing and Spiritual Enlightenment. Discover what the future holds for you and how to find your way along the path to inner peace and contentment. Ring Sapphire on the number below.'

Spike took out his notebook and wrote down the contact number. He was used to taking a punt on an outsider, telling himself that he could make his excuses if it turned out to be a waste of time, or if the services proved to be more physical than spiritual, though that might make an even better story.

There was a phone box on the other side of the road, so he made his way across and dialed the number, coin in hand waiting for the sound of a voice on the other end. It took a few rings before it was answered, and the woman sounded out of breath.

"Is that Sapphire?" asked Spike as the coin clattered into the box inside the base of the phone.

"Yes. How can I help?"

She sounded cultured, refined even. "I saw your card in the shop window and it interested me. I'd like to find out more. Can I come and see you?"

"I was just on my way out. I heard the phone as I was closing the door and dashed back inside to answer it. I'm working behind the bar at the Horse & Barge at lunchtimes. I'll be in there for a couple of hours if you want to come along."

"Ah, a different kind of spiritual enlightenment."

"It's just to tide me over in the quieter times. I'd better go or I'll be late. Maybe see you later."

Spike was just enjoying the prospect of being able to combine a lunchtime drink while legitimately following up a possible story when he heard the distant sound of a siren. Experience had taught him the difference in tonal urgency between the kind made by police cars, fire engines and ambulances, and he guessed that this was indeed an ambulance, a good chasing prospect.

He skipped smartly across the road to his car and had the engine running before the emergency vehicle had drawn level with him, pulling out behind it and tailing it down the road. It made several left and right turns, into a more built-up area, suggesting to Spike from the size of the roads that it must be nearing its destination.

In a quiet cul de sac of detached houses it slowed as it came towards a small group of people standing on one of the driveways. Judging by the slippers and light clothing being worn, it looked as if they had come out of their houses in response to the emergency.

Pulling up a few yards from the ambulance, Spike made his way towards the group, which was gathered around a figure lying on the ground. It was only when he got close that he could see a postman's uniform.

The ambulance staff were examining his leg, and a collapsible stretcher was being brought out to lift him off the ground. Spike sidled up to one of the bystanders, a woman wearing an apron and with traces of flour on her hands. "What happened?" he asked.

The woman glanced his way before looking back at the casualty. "It looks as if he's got a broken leg. He tripped over a plant pot in the front garden."

"Is the owner around?"

"That's him in the brown jumper."

Spike manoeuvred himself towards a pensioner standing near the front door watching the activity. "Unfortunate accident by the look of it," Spike offered.

"That's what happens when you try to take a short cut across the garden to save a few seconds." He had lowered his voice, but his words still reached the man in uniform on the ground.

"You put it there on purpose. If you've bust my leg you'll pay for it to get mended." He grimaced in pain as he was lifted on to the padded surface of the trolley.

"Can you prove that, 'cos if not that's slander?"

"You've been going on about your precious garden being trampled on for weeks. This is your revenge, but my solicitor will soon wipe your smile away."

The medical staff lifted the trolley and carried it to the ambulance, the small crowd of neighbours following it. Spike had his notebook out, jotting down what each person had said.

"What's that for?" asked the homeowner.

"I'm from the *Bartown Chronicle*. Sounds as if you feel strongly about what's happened, as if you've been hard done by. Can I use your name in the report?"

"Charles Appleby. He'll probably change his mind when he's had a chance to think it over. He'll come to his senses and realise he made a mistake." He pointed towards the large terracotta flowerpot, now lying on its side. "You can see where he's tried to go, across the flowerbed and the lawn, instead of going back the way he came, on the front drive, just to cut off the corner to my next-door neighbour's. People ought to have more respect."

He began to look a bit less certain about his situation. "Sounds as if you've had a bit of a running battle with him," Spike suggested.

"We've had a few cross words. It takes time and effort to get a garden looking nice, and just one person in a big pair of boots to spoil it."

"Will you take him on in court?"

"It won't come to that. He's got too much to lose to take it any further."

The ambulance was leaving and the neighbours drifting away. Spike pocketed his notebook and thanked Mr Appleby for his time. He handed him a business card with his contact number. "If you hear anything, let me know. I'll be interested to find out what happens."

Chapter 3

The Horse & Barge pub was on Spike's way back to the office, so he went straight there. The car park was about half full, and inside the low door there was a steady hum of conversation from the groups of drinkers spread around the main bar room.

Three people behind the bar were being kept busy serving drinks and taking orders for lunch. He recognised the landlord from occasional previous visits, and of the two women helping him he guessed that the older of the two was probably his part-time psychic healer.

He waited until she was free before making his approach. "Would you be Sapphire?" he asked.

She turned towards him. "Yes. You must be the caller."

"You really are psychic," he joked.

He could see that she was trying not to smile, but not succeeding entirely. "I recognised your voice."

He ordered a drink and chatted while she fetched it. She seemed like someone he could talk to, and someone with a story to tell. "Business must be slow to take a second job?"

"It fluctuates. Word of mouth often brings a flurry of interest, and then it wanes when people go on holiday. Working here helps me over the slack times."

"I may be able to help you there. I work for the *Bartown Chronicle*, and I thought perhaps a story in there about what you do could attract a bit of business."

She looked slightly disappointed. "I thought you were a customer when you rang."

"Maybe I could be. We could all do with a bit of inner contentment. Have you got a moment to talk?"

She looked at her boss struggling to keep up with the customers waiting to be served. "We've got a group booking in, that's why it's so busy," she explained. The girl on her other side was less occupied. "Karen, can you cover for me just for two minutes. I promise I'll be straight back."

Spike knew that he would have to arrange another time to do a full interview, but he was keen to get a flavour of what she might be willing to talk about, enough for a small story with a photo or maybe even a feature. There was a table free next to the door leading to the staff area, so he followed Sapphire there, drink in hand.

He took a seat directly opposite her, but he had only just lowered himself onto it when she said suddenly: "Don't sit there!"

He looked around him in surprise, as if he had missed something that she had seen. He must have given her a puzzled look because she continued. "Really. Don't sit there."

Slowly and reluctantly, he lifted himself off the stool and came further around the table nearer to where she was sitting. He wanted to say something lighthearted, to ease the awkwardness of being told rather brusquely what to do. But before he could come up with something, the door to the staff area swung open and a waitress carrying a tray containing a pot of coffee and several cups and saucers barged through, stubbing her foot. The coffee pot tumbled, emptying most of its contents over the stool where Spike had been sitting, splashing them both lightly with some of the droplets.

The waitress was full of apologies, pulling a cloth from her pocket to mop up while clearing the debris. Sapphire and Spike were on their feet, dusting themselves down.

The noise brought conversation in the pub to a halt for a moment, until everyone had identified the cause, and then slowly it resumed, but it was enough to make Sapphire realise that she was needed back at work. "I'd better go back behind the bar," she told him. "I need this job, to keep afloat."

"Can I come and see you at home, where we can have a longer chat, and maybe bring a photographer with me?" He'd seen enough to know that there was something here worthy of his attention, and his interest had been piqued to find out more.

He arranged a time that suited them both later in the week and wrote down her address. The waitress was still moping up the remains of the coffee with a bowl of water and a sponge as Sapphire went back behind the bar and Spike went outside to finish his drink on the tables in front of the pub, next to the road, which were now bathed in sunshine.

He had taken only a couple of appreciative pulls on his beer when a figure from inside the pub made his way unsteadily towards him, an almost full pint in his hand.

He stood for a moment beside the bench and smiled at Spike, in a way that only those who have had their share of the cares of the world lifted temporarily from their shoulders by liquid refreshment can.

"This seat taken?" asked the new arrival.

"Help yourself," said Spike, taking another swig in an effort to finish his drink sooner than he had planned, aware that he might need to make an exit if the newcomer became a nuisance.

"I saw you writing stuff down in a notebook in there," said the man. "You a reporter or summat?"

"Something like that, yes."

"That must be interesting."

"It has its moments."

"I could have been a reporter. I was good at writing at school. Always got top marks for my essays."

"Why didn't you?" asked Spike, not really interested in the reply.

"Didn't get the grades I needed in my exams. Didn't get to college. Applied for a few jobs but never got anywhere. Ended up in a factory, always wondering what I could have been."

"It's not as exciting as it looks," Spike confided. "If you saw some of the things I had to do, you would wish you were back in the factory."

"Oh, yeah? What sort of things?"

"Like when someone gets killed in a car accident and you have to go and talk to their partner or their mum and dad. You're sitting there while they're crying in front of you, and all you can think about is how to choose the right moment to ask them for a picture of the person who's died, to go in the paper."

"I wouldn't fancy that."

"It's part of the job. People hanging themselves, road crash victims, even an occasional murder."

The man paused for a moment, as if weighing up what he was about to say before saying it. "I've got a story for you."

Spike was getting near to the end of his drink, and was becoming grateful that he was only a couple of swigs away from leaving. Before he could say anything to encourage or discourage his companion, the man said: "I'm going to kill someone."

Spike let the statement hang in the air while he considered a suitable reply. "Have you been drinking?"

"Seriously. I'm being serious."

Humouring the man seemed like the best policy. "Just anyone, or have you got someone in particular in mind?"

"My teacher."

Spike let a slight smile play on his lips. "Aren't you a bit old to be still at school?"

"Don't laugh at me. You aren't writing this down," he said, taking umbrage at Spike's lack of interest.

"I've got a good memory."

"I've just seen one of my old teachers. He always had it in for me at school. Made me look stupid in front of the class by asking me the hardest questions, told my mum and dad that I would never do anything worthwhile when they went to see him. Then when I took my exams, we had to do a project and he got to mark it. Everything else got sent away to be marked, but unless you got a pass for the project you couldn't get a grade in the main exam. He failed my project, so I failed the whole thing, and it was all because of him. Everything that's happened since was all down to him. That was years ago. I thought he'd moved away, but then I saw him out walking. I followed him. He didn't see me. So, when the time's right, when I'm good and ready, it'll be payback time. Write down my phone number. You'll need it when it happens."

Spike finished his drink and stood up, taking his notebook out for the man to dictate the number to him. "What did you say your name was?" he asked.

"I didn't."

"Ah, the man with no name. Like in the spaghetti westerns." Spike took a final look at his face. "Adios amigo," and he put his notebook back in his pocket and headed for his car to drive back to the office.

When Spike arrived, Carl was in the reporters' room with the young freelance photographer that the paper used to illustrate most of its stories, having no full-time one. It was rare for her to be in the office, but she and Carl had just returned from a job and she had accepted his offer of a cup of tea before going on her way, it being almost the weekend.

"Ah this is the man who can give the casting vote," said Carl as Spike walked in. "Kat says I'm fat…"

"No I didn't," she interjected, but Carl ignored her.

"Kat says I'm fat, on account of the fact that I don't exercise, but I know I'm just normal weight."

"What I said was that maybe you could take a leaf out of the book of the man you've just interviewed and have a try at jogging."

"In other words, I'm overweight."

Kat sighed and turned to Spike. "We've just been to see someone who took part in that London Marathon thing they've just held and the guy said a year ago he'd never done any exercise, but now he can run twenty-six miles."

Carl wasn't persuaded. "So, you're saying that on cold winter's nights when I finish work and it's chucking it down and pitch dark, instead of going home to a nice warm house and a hot meal I should change into shorts and a vest and go loping along the pavement in plimsolls like some of the herberts I've seen? I'd rather chop my leg off and donate it to medical science. I think I'll just die of lethargy, if it's all the same to you."

Kat rolled her eyes, as Spike asked what the man got for his recent achievement.

"A bit of metal to hang around his neck and show his friends for a while until it ends up in the back of his sock drawer to never see the light of day again." Carl was warming to his theme. "Mark my words, it's just a fad, this jogging craze. I give it five years, six at most, by which time sensible people will have realised what a hassle it is and it'll have fizzled out, like streaking at football matches, and those vans with loud hailers on the roof telling people to vote on poling day."

"Don't worry," said Spike. "We'll come to your funeral to make sure you get a decent send-off."

But Carl had been searching his head for a suitable quotation rather than listening to what his colleague was saying, calling on his knowledge of English literature to enhance his argument. When he found it, he stood up, the better to enunciate, his words accompanied by a dramatic sweep of his hand.

"As the Bard put it," he declared. "'Let me have men about me that are fat: Sleek-headed men and such as sleep o' nights; Yond' Cassius has a lean and hungry look; He thinks too much: such men are dangerous.'"

Kat knew when she was beaten, or at least wasting her breath trying to get Carl to see the error of his ways, so she finished her tea and picked up her camera bag. She knew that Carl, for all his stubbornness, could also be entertaining, but she had film to develop and prints to be made. "I'll get the pictures of the marathon man through to you. I'll drop them in on the way to the job with Spike." She glanced towards Spike. "See you at the court on Monday."

By the time that Spike had finished re-writing the reports sent in by correspondents that Tom had left him, he was ready to go home. Home to Spike these days was a downstairs room in a large house belonging to a family of four, who used the small income from the rent he paid, for what was effectively a bed-sit, to offset their bills. He also had a small kitchen, off the main one used by the family, with a back door that led to the garden and provided his main access in and out of the property around the side of the house.

An outside loo with a shower in a small brick building in the garden meant he didn't need to venture upstairs, though when winter brought a run of frosts, he had to boil a kettle and take it out with him to defrost the ice in the toilet pan.

It was a long way from the time when he'd had his own house and his own mortgage, but while those days had been more comfortable, they had also brought misery. All things considered he was happier this way. When he put something down, he knew where to find it, and he could choose how he spent his spare time, what he ate and drank and when and where, without having to explain or justify his actions. The older he got, the more he valued simplicity.

There was a note on the kitchen worktop when he came through the back door, telling him that the owners of the house, the Barratt family, had gone away for the school holidays. It meant he had two weeks of tranquillity; no piano practises, noisy films on television or loud conversations would be coming through the walls.

The price was a small one. In return for this splendid isolation, he was being asked to feed the family's cat, a large docile creature of uncertain gender with long brown fur, named Slug on account of its lethargy. It seemed to find nothing worthy of haste, neither the prospect of food nor the lure of the garden's bird population, but seemed content to loaf about so long as its bowls of water and dried cat food were kept topped up in the family's kitchen on a regular basis.

The note from the Barratts carried a P.S. Some leftovers had been offloaded by Mrs Barratt from her fridge to Spike's on the off-chance that he might like to use them up in the family's absence. However, no clue as to what they were had been given.

Always up for a challenge, Spike peeled the lid off a Tupperware bowl and contemplated the thick pink goo inside with a sense of misgiving, wondering whether it could be sweet or savoury. He tried half a spoonful, expecting to recognise it and gauge from its taste whether it needed to be heated prior to being eaten, but it tasted of nothing.

He weighed up the alternative meal possibilities within his cupboards, which were no more inviting, and decided to eat it as it was, hoping that nothing untoward happened to him in the hours that followed.

With both himself and Slug fed, he went out into the garden to enjoy the last of the day's sunshine. Through the open door behind him he could hear the crunching of feline nuggets enriched with real chicken and rabbit. It had looked to Spike much like cat litter, which fortunately wasn't something he needed to deal with in his duties, since the family had sawed a rectangular hole in the bottom of the back door with a power tool and fitted a cat flap.

Spike sat on the patio, contemplating the freedom of the weekend. The birds flitted back and forth across the garden and hopped across the lawn, perhaps also aware of what the crunching noise coming from inside the house implied in terms of their safety and freedom of movement.

When he wasn't asked to work a weekend, covering the fairs, fêtes and carnivals that provided regular public attractions in the town throughout the spring and summer, Spike would sometimes drive the sixty or so miles to the city where he grew up, to visit his parents, which is what he planned to do this weekend.

They were now in their late seventies, and Spike was aware each time he went that one day he would be making the journey for a different reason, when one of them had passed away.

It was always strange, returning to the streets that were once a part of his daily life, seemingly familiar and unfamiliar at the same time. Everywhere there were memories – the corner shop where he'd bought sweets, now converted into a home for someone; the trees where he'd collected conkers to take to school; and the blind junction on the side of a hill where cars coming around the corner quickly on the main road were upon you just as you struggled to get enough speed up to get across safely from a standing start on your bike.

He parked in the driveway and let himself in the front door, using the same key that he had kept attached to his purse back in his school days when he had got the bus home.

His mother was in the kitchen preparing food, and she dried her hands on a towel hanging from the handle of the oven door before coming and giving him a hug as a welcome. To her he would always be Stephen, and hearing his given name was part of the accompanying journey back in time to when his main concerns had been doing his homework and remembering to pack all the items of sports kit he needed to take with him to school the next morning. They sat at the dining table and talked for a while, until his father joined them from his gardening duties, his mother then finishing making the meal.

There was a reassuring familiarity about everything in their home, little having changed since it had been his as well. The ornaments on the shelves, souvenirs from holidays abroad, the pictures on the walls, one painted by a relative, and the photographs on the windowsills, including one of him and his brother, taken by his father, dusted dutifully every week and returned to the space where it belonged.

Even the questions that his mother asked were familiar. How was work going? Was he looking after himself? Had he met any nice young ladies? His answers were just as predictable, but the ritual of asking and answering was performed with good grace, like a ceremonial dance performed on the occasions of his visits, to fulfill the obligation of continuing the routine.

For Spike, it was a chance to shed his load for a few hours and leave behind his responsibilities, becoming carefree for a while, until his car bonnet was pointed in the direction of Bartown once more and his former life receded in the rear-view mirror.

It served as a safety net, knowing that if his world fell in on him, he had a place to which he could escape, and even if he didn't use it, just having it there was a reassurance of somewhere to hide, despite his parents' advancing years. Perhaps it made it easier for him to take risks, knowing that the door to his old life was still partly open, welcoming him back, though every time he returned, he could see that the gap left by the open door behind him had narrowed a little further. The familiar sign beside the road that said 'Welcome to Bartown' was where he shed his former life and became an adult once more.

Returning on Sunday night, Spike thought how it was his turn for covering the town's magistrates' court in the morning, and among the cases due to be heard was one involved a certain Darren Rumsey. The advantage of knowing in advance when he would be facing Mr Rumsey once again was that he could be ready for what he thought might happen.

Chapter 4

The following morning, as Spike started his car and prepared to drive away, pulling out the choke to combat the low temperature, he was aware of another car coming alongside his. It stopped next to him, and the driver turned towards him, his window already down. Spike thought he was going to be asked for directions, but when he looked at the driver's face, he could see that the man had more on his mind than just help in finding a destination.

He had what Spike called a 'sunken' face, the sort that showed the shape and contours of his skull beneath the thin covering of skin, and eyes that seemed unnaturally close together. There was a company name decorating the bonnet, showing that the man behind the wheel was a taxi driver.

Spike leaned across and wound down his passenger-side window, looking back up at the man when he'd done so, hoping that the features had improved to show a lighter mood, correcting the first impression that Spike had been given. They hadn't.

"You shouldn't be parking here," the man told him. "You'm not a resident."

Spike registered surprise, tempered by an awareness that he didn't have time for an argument. He had work commitments to fulfil, so he restricted his answer to a factual one, rather than asking why the man had reached that conclusion.

"I am a resident. I live here."

It didn't have the desired effect.

"I know the family what lives here," he replied, flicking his eyes in the direction of the house where Spike rented his room. "You'm not one of 'em."

Spike looked at his watch. He needed to be away. It seemed to make the taxi driver similarly aware that time was passing, and with it his potential for earning fares. "Just a warning to you," he said, rounding off his message. "So's you know."

With that the car pulled away, the driver giving Spike a final malevolent glance as he went on his way down the street. Spike waited for him to disappear before he pulled away. At least now he could get to where he needed to be. The problem of where he could and couldn't park in future and why not could wait for another time.

Bartown Magistrates' Court was designed with the same quirk of layout favoured by many in the UK in that the press bench was positioned right alongside the dock. This meant that when the members of the Bench retired to consider their verdict, the perpetrators of the crime that they were considering were left twiddling their thumbs just a couple of feet away from a member of the press, whose intention was to tell everyone in the local area the full details of their misdemeanour.

Unsurprisingly, many of those waiting to be sentenced took the opportunity to try to avoid having their shame spread across the pages of the paper, whether by persuasion or, more usually, by issuing threats.

So it was that Spike found himself just a short distance away from Darren Rumsey, whose vest and some of his tattoos were now hidden beneath a suit, a shirt with a starched white collar and a tie. All looked as if they were fresh out of their packaging, while the collar bit into its new owner's neck like the ones used to restrain his powerful dogs.

"Don't I know you from somewhere?" asked Darren leaning over the edge of the wooden surround to peer down on Spike seated at the desk just below in the near-empty courtroom, everyone else having drifted outside for a cigarette or a chat, to await the call to return when the magistrates reappeared.

"I'm always being told that," said Spike, trying to look busy with his notes.

"Yeah, I know you. Weren't you the guy from round the corner, said you'd seen a reporter knocking on doors?"

"Maybe you're confusing me with someone else."

But there was no fooling Mr Rumsey. "I remember you now. You lied to me." There was a pause while the import of what he had said sank in. Then he added: "This had better not be going in the paper."

Spike had covered enough court cases to have been in this situation before, and he had the stock answers that all who find themselves faced with intimidation are taught to trot out in their defence.

"It's not up to me whether it appears in the paper, it's down to the editor," Spike informed him.

"Yeah, but you're writing it. You could leave it out if you wanted and no one would know."

"The editor gets to see the court sheet and wants to know what happened in each case. He would know that something was missing. Besides, the public have a right to know."

"Yeah, just like I've got the right to teach you a lesson."

There was a noise of a door opening in the corner of the room and the chairman of the Bench reappeared, followed by her two fellow magistrates. The court usher, who had been lingering near the exit, signaled to those outside to retake their seats as the session was about to resume.

"The court will rise!" he bellowed in his best town crier voice, and everyone dutifully obeyed, including Spike and the defendant.

The members of the Bench seated themselves and then the lady magistrate, in the centre of the trio, turned to address Darren Rumsey.

"We have carefully considered your explanation in answer to the charge of possession of two dangerous dogs, and in light of your reassurances that you will keep them on leads both in your garden and when in public areas, and taking into consideration your previous good character, and the fact that you haven't owned the dogs for very long and were learning how to handle them, we feel prepared to impose a conditional discharge in this case, for a period of one year, to allow you to show your willingness to atone for what happened with a period of good behaviour. Do you understand what that means?"

"Yes, your honour," said Darren, dutifully.

"Do you have licences for both of your dogs?"

"Yes, your honour."

"In that case you are free to go, while ensuring that a similar incident never happens again."

"Thank you, your honour," said Darren, stepping down from the dock and making his way out of court while the magistrates moved on to the next case on the agenda.

It was only after several rather uninteresting further cases involving non-payment of television licence fees and driving without road tax and insurance had been heard that the session came to an end and Spike was free to leave.

He filed out of the court alongside the rest of the small crowd, which included members of the public who had been in the gallery and friends and relatives of those whose cases had just been heard.

Across the car park he spotted a familiar figure, a young woman with shoulder-length dark hair and around her neck a large camera with an even larger flashgun attached. As he reached the steps of the court he caught her eye, but he stopped without acknowledging her fully. He looked around the car park, watching the last few people from inside drift away. For a moment he thought he had misjudged the moment, but then he heard it, that same scraping of claws on tarmac that he had heard before, and he saw the two dogs racing towards him from the other side of the road, where Darren Rumsey had parked his grey van.

Spike sprinted to his car just as the dogs came for him, and though the damage to his clothing as the first one launched itself at his back meant sacrificing his favourite jacket, the pictures that Kat took from her carefully chosen vantage point were worth it to go with his story.

"We make a good team, you and me," he said to her afterwards, sitting in his car when the dogs and their owner had fled the scene. "Me as dog food to bait the trap and you springing it shut."

"I don't think I've ever photographed a reporter being attacked before," she said, watching him trying to repair the hole in his jacket. There was always something that he found reassuring in her soft Scottish accent.

"It won't be the last time, I can assure you," he told her. He examined the rip in his jacket. "You know what Carl would say. 'Dog bites man isn't a story; man bites dog, now that's a story!'"

———

20

He finally abandoned his feeble attempts to join the sides of the hole. "I didn't just bring you here to take pictures of me. There's a woman that I've arranged to interview this afternoon, a psychic healer. If you follow me in your car I'll take you to her place, so that when you've got some shots of her, you'll have your car and be able to get on your way."

Spike almost missed the entrance to the address he had been given by Sapphire. He had been driving slowly along the main road looking at the house numbers but often finding none. When he did eventually see the one that he wanted, the number painted on one of two old stone columns framing the grand front door, he had to bump the wheels of his car up the steep kerb of the pavement to reach the gravel drive, which suggested that the old house had been built before cars had come along.

Kat parked behind him and while she fetched her camera gear from the boot, he looked at the display of buttons with name tags alongside for each of the flats, feeling a little disappointed that the woman he had come to see wasn't the sole occupier of the building.

He found the button he needed and gave it a press, and a few seconds later a buzz and a click from the door indicated that they were being let in.

As they climbed the staircase, noticing the ornate corbels in the form of stone faces looking down at them from the foot of the arches, they could hear voices echoing from a few flights above. Two people were talking, and it became evident that the previous client was being bid farewell. The words 'peace and blessings' carried down to the new arrivals, and then a woman with a supermarket shopping bag in one hand and her car keys in the other passed them on her way down, smiling politely as they stepped aside.

On the second floor they found Sapphire waiting beside her open front door. She invited them inside, and Spike introduced his photographer colleague on their way past. Sapphire noticed him looking around the main room, and as she offered them seats in the armchairs she said: "You were probably expecting surroundings a bit more gothic, maybe with a black cat watching your every move."

"I think I pictured more of a hippy feel to things, perhaps a joss stick or two burning in the background, maybe a wind chime hanging next to an open window."

"Sorry to disappoint you," she said.

"No, it's maybe more intriguing this way."

Kat busied herself with her camera equipment and began taking a few profile pictures of their host while she and Spike talked, moving around behind him to get different angles. She asked Sapphire if she would mind sitting at a table next to the window for a few moments, so that she could use the natural daylight to light her subject, and moved a vase of flowers into the background to balance the picture. When she had taken a selection of images, some in close up, some from a distance to show the surroundings, her subject looking at the camera and then away, she told Spike that she had enough photos.

When she had gone, he was just deciding how best to begin the questioning when Sapphire asked him: "What happened to your jacket?"

Spike glanced self-consciously over his shoulder. "Oh, yes. The previous job. Someone set their dogs on me. People aren't always pleased to see us in this profession."

"Take it off and I'll mend it for you while we talk."

There was something about the calmness of her voice that made obedience compulsory. She saw him looking a little awkward. "Really," she said, and held out her hands. With the jacket across her knees, she took a needle and thread from a bag beside her chair and began sewing.

"I thought it was people that you mended, not their clothing."

"In some ways they are very similar, you just need to know how it's done. Tell me," she asked, "is it solely business that has brought you here or are there more personal reasons?"

"To be honest, it's a bit of both."

"It's always best to be honest. Problems are only made worse by dishonesty."

"I was intrigued by what I read on your card."

"In what way?"

"The idea that you can tell someone's future, and that people can come to you to find guidance and healing."

"Everyone sees a different message when they read that card. In their mind they see what they hope to find, the answers and the certainty."

"Can you really know about people just by looking at them?" he asked.

"I know from looking at you that you have some mental scars that have never healed. Memories of conversations with your parents, things that you said and wished you hadn't, but now can't forget. And your ex-wife. When people ask you now why you have never remarried, you answer: 'Once bitten, twice shy.' But it goes deeper than that, doesn't it? There are things that you learnt about yourself that you don't want to revisit. Better to close that box and vow never to lift the lid again."

Spike tried to deflect the line of thought away from himself. He asked her: "But what about the future? It would be remarkable to be able to tell people what's going to happen to them."

"But it's often not what they want to hear. They may think they want to know, but that's because they are expecting good news. If they learn that they will always be poor, that their marriage will end in divorce or that they don't have long to live, they wish they hadn't asked, because what can be learnt in a second can also never be forgotten. You must be careful what you wish for; it is often not what you expect."

"How did you get involved in this line of work?"

"I've always been able to read people, even as a child. I could see the ones who were looking for a friend, and the ones who wanted to hurt me. So, I helped people with their problems, and it grew from there."

"But how did you help people?"

"By listening to them, listening to what they said, but more importantly what they didn't say. We leave out the parts that we don't want people to see in us. That's why I said it's always best to be honest. And I show them how to let go, to let go of guilt and allow themselves to heal. People need to be given permission to move on, to leave bad memories behind. They need to hear it from someone that it's okay. I'm just the person who tells them that, because nobody else does."

"Your name, Sapphire, is that your business name?"

"No, it's on my birth certificate. My parents told me they chose it because it represents protection and strength. I was very weak when I was born, and they didn't know whether I would survive. So, when I did, they named me after one of the strongest of precious stones."

She cut the thread on Spike's jacket and handed it back to him. He examined the place where the hole had been, and even running his finger across it he couldn't find the spot where the repair had been made.

"Wow! I was thinking I'd have to throw it away, which would have been a shame. It's one that I wear a lot."

"Never give up on something you love."

"Perhaps I should mention in the article that clients can bring their clothes along to be mended at the same time."

"Maybe not. I don't want to be knee deep in old laundry."

As he stood at the door of his car, he looked up at the window two floors above, overlooking the road, and saw her there, watching and waiting. He told himself that this was why he enjoyed being a journalist, the interesting people and the unpredictable nature of the work. You never quite knew what was coming around the next corner.

Chapter 5

There was an unfamiliar face in the reporters' room when Spike pushed the door open and walked inside. Tom and Carl were there, as usual, but seated at a new desk against the far wall was a man in a smart suit and shiny, black, pointy-toed shoes. Spike's desk had been moved along the wall a little to accommodate the new arrival, who was busying himself arranging items in the drawers from a large cardboard box and positioning his typewriter and phone.

"Ah, Spike. Let me introduce you to Harry," said Tom. "He's a reporter with the *Evening Post* who is going to be based here in the office for the foreseeable future." Spike offered his hand, but for a moment the newcomer was unloading the last of his items. Spike's hand hovered there waiting to be acknowledged, which a few seconds later it was, accompanied by a weak smile.

The positioning of Spike's desk meant he was now facing the new man, whose desk was sideways on to his. This meant that whatever he was doing, writing a story or talking on the phone, he would be looking at the man from the *Evening Post*, a rival for stories in a sleepy town where newsworthy items were hard to find. And daily deadlines meant anything that came his way would be gobbled up and printed and wrapped around fish and chips or used to line bird cages long before the weekly *Bartown Chronicle* presses had even been inked up ready for action.

"What you working on? Anything interesting?" asked Harry.

The question confirmed Spike's worst fears, that the office was no longer a safe haven where stories could be discussed and debated prior to being delivered. Now there was a spy in the camp, and every word spoken, every line typed and every phone call would have to be considered closely with secrecy in mind. The fact that Tom was standing nearby, also interested in his answer, made things even more difficult. He needed to show the latter person that he had been busy, while not creating too much interest in the mind of the former.

"Just a court case from this morning and a feature from this afternoon."

"Would that be the dangerous dog man?"

More bad news. He was up to speed on what was going on already, and probably asked the question expecting that answer. "Yes."

"Could you knock out a short piece for us on the dog man for the late additions? Is there a picture of him?"

It was almost as if he could see inside Spike's head. "Our freelance photographer has a few shots of him."

"Is that Kat?"

Spike kept trying to stop saying: 'Oh, dear' to himself every time he heard Harry speak, but it was becoming impossible. He felt like one of those insects that you see rushing for cover when you lift a brick off the ground and their entire world is suddenly open to the skies. "Yes."

"I need to give her a ring anyway, to introduce myself. I'll get her to send a couple of pics across to go with your story."

He glanced at his watch. "Oops! Better go. Got a local bigwig to butter up over a bite to eat and a drink or two. See you later." He tucked a new notebook into his pocket and a couple of pens and strode out, the breeze lifting a few pieces of loose paper on a nearby desk, to flutter back down when he had gone, leaving just a faint whiff of aftershave behind him.

Tom looked at Spike, who looked at Carl, who looked back at Tom, and for a moment none of them spoke. "Maybe it won't be for long," said Tom eventually. "If he can't come up with enough material to justify the cost of having him here, the powers that be may reel him back in."

But he couldn't hide the tone of wishful thinking in his voice. There was an air of change in the office that had a permanent feel about it.

"He seems like a decent sort of bloke," Carl said hopefully. "As the saying goes, 'Keep your friends close and your enemies closer.' He probably won't be in the office much of the time anyway, and we send stuff over to them already, so it might not feel any different when we get used to it."

"How did it go with your psychic woman?" asked Tom. "Did you find enlightenment?"

"I think I'll need another lifetime for that," Spike told him. "But she had some interesting things to say. I'll knock it out while it's quiet and I don't have to put my arm around my work to stop the kid at the next desk copying. At least I know where I can get help now if things go downhill further."

As Spike parked his car when he got home, he looked up and down the road for any sign of the taxi that had drawn alongside him at the start of the day, without success. There were cars parked on both sides of the road, reducing the amount of space available, but with still enough room available for those who needed it and had still to return home.

On the previous evening there had been more cars than usual, visitors to a gathering in one of the houses nearby, and Spike had taken the only free space. He decided he would leave earlier than usual the next morning, partly to avoid a similar confrontation with the man with the sunken face, and partly in case there was another delay and he needed to have time to spare.

He was glad he had when he saw the same taxi waiting for him to come out to his car, double parked across him as before. He steeled himself for a similar verbal exchange again this morning, hoping that seeing him walking along the drive of the home where he had a room would be enough to demonstrate that he lived there, but the taxi was empty. Not only that, but also the engine wasn't running. Spike realised that it had been positioned there to block him in and prevent him from going on his way.

He stood beside his car, weighing up the options, aware that he was almost certainly being watched, depending upon where the taxi driver lived. Public transport was one alternative, but he needed his car to get around, and there would be no guarantee that the taxi would be gone if he came back later, if the man had arranged a day off.

He looked at the distance between his car and the ones behind and in front, and figured that with a bit of backwards and forwards manoeuvring he may be able to get enough of an angle on his car to back it up the kerb onto the pavement and then squeeze between the car in front and the bumper of the taxi.

He decided to give it a try, travelling just a few inches in first gear and then reversing a few inches until he had turned the car enough so that he could lift the rear nearside wheel onto the kerb and steer the back of his car onto the pavement, all the time looking around in case the owner of the other vehicle reappeared.

There wasn't a lot to spare between his paintwork and that of the other cars, but by getting out and checking his progress on both sides, he was able to squeeze through and get away. Only the heavy feeling of knowing that he might have to do it all again the following morning detracted from the feeling of elation at successfully negotiating a way out of the jam.

One of Spike's duties at the start of each day involved contacting the local police station to find out whether anything newsworthy had happened overnight. Sometimes he carried out his 'police calls' job by ringing from the office, if he had another morning appointment, but at other times he would call in person and speak to the desk sergeant on duty when he arrived.

This morning he had time to make his way there, and so pulled up alongside the few other vehicles in the row of bays allocated to the visiting public. As he walked towards the entrance, he noticed a red MGB sports car parked at the end of the row, with a personalised number plate that began with the letters FHD followed by 1A. He remembered how in his younger days he had whiled away the hours on long journeys making up words beginning with each of the letters of number plates, like Roald Dahl's Big Friendly Giant.

He skipped up the half a dozen steps to the doors and once inside rang the bell on the counter for assistance, as requested on the sign alongside. A large officer in shirtsleeves ambled in, not one that he had seen before, and Spike introduced himself.

"Nothing for the press," was the somewhat curt reply. Spike let the notebook that he had been lifting out of his pocket drop back inside.

"Really?" he said, not disguising his disappointment. "Nothing at all?" He was hoping for at least a sympathetic tone, followed by a short explanation that it had been a quiet evening and night, but all he got was a repeat of the former message.

"Nothing for the press."

Spike shrugged and turned away, surprised to be back outside so soon. He had been considering mentioning the parking problems that he was having, but the stony-faced response that he got from his initial enquiry dissuaded him from doing so.

He sat in his car for a few moments, working out what to do next now that he didn't have any leads to follow up in the office. He heard voices from the other side of the car park, and looking in his wing mirror he saw two figures shaking hands warmly in farewell amid jovial exchanges and then a: "Thanks again. See you later," from the man leaving, while the other, his shirt bearing the shoulder stripes of a senior officer, went back inside. Spike recognised him as Chief Inspector James Parish, and his newfound friend was the man he would be facing in the office from now on, *Evening Post* reporter Harry Dixon.

The red sports car's engine roared into life, and Harry zipped out of the car park, eager to get things moving on his first full day based in the office of the *Bartown Chronicle*.

Spike was pleased to see that the car wasn't parked in the main road outside the *Chronicle* office. It would give him a chance to talk to the others about what he had just seen.

"I could be wrong, but I got a feeling that the desk sergeant had been primed not to tell me anything," he told them. "It's one thing for Harry to cream off the best stories, but if he's going to stop us getting all the lesser ones as well, we're going to struggle to fill the paper."

Tom was half sitting on one of the desks, puffing thoughtfully on his pipe. Seeing him with it always reminded Spike of the first time that he had met him, at the interview for the job of reporter, which he had seen in a copy of the industry trade magazine *UK Press Gazette*. He had heard the phrase 'pipe and slippers' in connection with people who had reached retirement age, but he had never seen someone employing both when working in an office. But Tom was partial to life's little comforts, changing back into his shoes when he needed to venture outside. All he needed was an old tweed jacket with brown leather elbows patches to complete the set.

"If there was something worthwhile on police calls this morning, Harry'll have to write it up for today's paper, and then we can confront him about cutting off our supply," Tom reasoned.

Carl was in his customary position, warming his hands in front of the gas fire beside his desk, a cigarette burning in the ashtray at his elbow. "He's gonna get the pick of the stories anyway with a daily deadline. He doesn't need to get to them first. I don't think it'll make a whole lot of difference."

"But what about him needing to satisfy his professional pride?" argued Spike. "He'll want to justify his appointment to the *Evening Post*. He hasn't been put here just to get us to send stuff across to them more often, he's here to get the best stories first and write them himself, and then leave us with the crumbs after he's finished. Up until now we've been able to keep a few things back for ourselves, to show that we aren't just a rehash of what the *Evening Post* has used already. But if he gets first pick of everything, anyone who reads both papers will think that ours isn't worth the bother."

Spike's gaze drifted to the empty chair and desk in front of him, and he wondered what its owner was up to at that moment.

"Leave it till the first editions of today's *Evening Post* come over on the van," reasoned Tom, "and we'll decide what to do then." He sauntered through to his office at the back of the reporters' room, leaving his colleagues to continue with their job of typing up wedding reports and agricultural show results, for which a good number of readers still bought the paper.

When the *Evening Post* arrived, on the courier van that shuttled between the two offices, ferrying words and pictures to staff at the main HQ and post and papers to the outlying areas, one of the women behind the counter cut the string that held the bundle together.

She brought copies through to the reporters, as she did every day, dropping them on a spare desk for when anyone interested got a moment to flick through the pages.

The sound of the papers landing on the surface brought Tom through from his office, and his two staff were already unfolding their copies. Tom flattened his broadsheet on the main desk in the reporters' room and read the front-page headline. Under the banner 'Exclusive!' it said: 'Fears grow for missing man'. The story below read: 'A manhunt has been launched for a pensioner last seen three days ago amid fears that he could have come to harm.

'Retired teacher Geoffrey Fellows left his home in Bartown last Saturday to visit a private area of woodland where he owns a writing hut.

'His wife, Isabelle, raised the alarm when he failed to return at the arranged time.

'"It is completely out of character for him to disappear like this," she told *Evening Post* reporter Harry Dixon. "He didn't take any money with him and had nothing except a small folder of writing notes."

'Police are appealing for anyone who thinks they may have seen Geoffrey Fellows in the past few days to get in touch.

'The former schoolmaster at Bartown College, who retired two years ago, is also the author of several non-fiction books.

'Chief Inspector James Parish urged: "We need to trace Mr Fellows as a matter of urgency. Anyone who can supply us with information regarding his whereabouts can do so in the knowledge that their identity will be treated in the strictest confidence."'

Alongside the story was a photo of Mr Fellows, a professional picture bearing the credit: 'Courtesy of Bartown College.'

The three finished reading at roughly the same time. Tom grimaced and Carl muttered a couple of swear words, which seemed to sum up the mood, but Spike was too shocked to say anything. He had a lot more to contemplate now than just office rivalry.

"He's got a bit of explaining to do," said Tom, finally. "Not that his bosses will be bothered. A front page exclusive on his first day in the job means they'll be patting him on the back. We'll need to find a new angle on the story. Spike, get in touch with the college and arrange to have a chat with the headmaster tomorrow morning, to get a bit of background detail, and the same with Mrs Fellows. There may be something that Harry has missed in his rush to make the early editions. With a bit of luck, the bloke will turn up safe and well, and we can trump their story by saying it was all a false alarm."

Back at home, Spike thought about parking further up the road to try to avoid another early morning confrontation, but a sense of injustice made him return to his usual place, though he gave himself a bit more room from the car behind, just in case. Why should he bow to a bully who was trying to impose his will without good reason? If he did, there would be no way back, and he would be inconvenienced on a daily basis. It looked as if a showdown was inevitable, in which case it was better to be ready for the man when it happened.

Once again, he made an early start just in case, and this time the man with the sunken face was standing waiting for him, his hands on his hips, staring down the drive as Spike approached.

"You'm haven't learnt your lesson, 'ave you," he told Spike, glaring already.

Spike stopped in front of him, wanting to get to the bottom of what was going on.

"What's your problem?" he asked, in what he hoped was a tone that reflected his genuine interest in hearing the man's objection to his parking location while also sounding firm enough to suggest that he wasn't in the mood to back down.

"You'm no business parking here. These spaces is for residents," the man said gruffly.

Spike made a show of looking up and down the road for parking signs and on the ground for yellow lines. "Where are the parking restrictions?" he asked, convinced in his mind that what he was asking sounded perfectly reasonable. "Where does it say I can't park here?"

The taxi driver took a step closer to him. "You'm not from round here, are you?" He looked Spike up and down. "I can tell from the way you speaks." As the penny began to drop with Spike, the man added: "You'd be best off goin' back to where you came from."

Spike had seen it coming. He had met people who had spent their whole lives in the town, hardly ever leaving it, perhaps travelling ten miles down the road just once in the previous decade, then talking about it as if they had been to the moon and back. It was like stepping back in time to an era where if you couldn't get somewhere on foot and home again the same day you didn't go there, ever. Driving outside the town boundaries was such an extraordinary thing to do, it seemed as if they were likely to fall off the edge of the world.

Spike didn't know whether to show dismay or pity. Instead, he said: "I'm here now, and that's all that matters."

But the taxi driver just said: "We'll see about that," as he walked away, leaving Spike to get in his car and drive off, a growing feeling of misgiving weighing on his mind.

Chapter 6

Bartown College had an imposing grandeur about it, with its sweeping lawns and wide stone steps funnelling visitors into the tall entrance area bordered by heavy wooden doors that were pinned open.

Suits and even school caps were the required uniform for pupils, while the headmaster, Robin Urquhart, wore a thin black gown over his grey suit, the hem of which fluttered behind him as he strode the corridors.

Spike walked with him through the grounds, their feet crunching on the gravel of the drive as they talked, amid the distant sound of teachers taking lessons while projecting their voices to reach the ears of those pupils seated in the furthest corners of the large classrooms.

"I haven't seen Geoffrey in a while," the headmaster told him. "He retired a couple of years ago, to tend his garden and write his books."

"What did he teach?" asked Spike.

"English Literature, up to 'O' Level standard. He also directed the school plays."

"Did he work here for long?"

"Eight or nine years. A final stint before he reached an age and pecuniary situation suitable to calling it a day."

"Did he get a big send-off?"

"I think there was a whip-round for a present, and a few of the staff who knew him best gathered for a glass of wine, but we didn't 'kill the fatted calf' for him. He hadn't been here long enough to merit that."

"Did he seem happy to be going?"

"I would say so. When you reach a certain age, the attraction of being able to plan your day around your various interests rather than the needs of the college and its pupils begins to outweigh the desire to pass on your knowledge to yet another year class of often reluctant minds, especially as the age gap between you and them increases with every year that you continue teaching."

"He'd had enough?"

"I don't think Geoffrey is the sort to feel at a loss at the prospect of a new day with no work commitments to fill it. He will have soon replaced his college activities with something of his own choosing."

"Was he popular? Did you ever get the impression that anyone resented him, maybe even bore him a grudge?"

"I don't know whether you are implying that he may have come to harm at the hands of someone here at the college, but there is no evidence to suggest that could be the case. Whatever has happened, we all hope and pray that he is found safe and well. There may be a perfectly plausible explanation for his absence, in which case we can all express our gratitude and put this episode behind us."

Spike bid the headmaster farewell and then drove to the home of the missing man's wife. On the outskirts of the town, he followed the directions that Geoffrey Fellows' wife had given him when he had called the number in the telephone directory and asked if he could visit her to help the cause of finding her husband by writing a piece for the *Bartown Chronicle*.

He found himself driving along a long, tree-lined avenue of tall, neatly clipped hedges with narrow driveways and large, private front gardens on either side. Counting his way in twos from the most prominent number on one of the front gates, he turned into the entrance of a large detached house behind a well-tended lawn surrounded by flowerbeds.

Isabelle Fellows was at the door already by the time he had reached it and invited him inside. She led the way into a sizeable living room with the sort of deep-pile carpet that sank as you walked on it, and offered him a seat in an armchair.

She seemed to Spike like someone who was determined to cope with whatever outcome came her way from her husband's disappearance. The neatness of their home suggested to him that she was organised and efficient in her duties, and that she would deal with this crisis in her life with a similar sense of purpose.

Spike asked her the standard questions that he was sure had been covered already by Harry Dixon on his visit, about when she last saw her husband, but which he knew he needed to ask to hear her replies first hand.

"It was on Saturday. Geoffrey went for a walk, as he always did after breakfast, saying that he would be back in time for lunch."

"You didn't go with him?"

"He has a hut where he likes to write, so I leave him to his creative flow. It's a routine that he follows. I would only be in his way, and there is plenty for me to do here, with the garden."

"Where is the hut?"

"It's less than a mile from here. Geoffrey bought a small area of woodland when it came up for sale, and got permission to have a wooden hut constructed on the site. It has no electricity or mains water, but he is only there for a few hours in the daytime, and it is quiet and secluded, and he can be free from interruptions, so it suits his purpose."

"How does he keep it secure?"

"He had a lock fitted and has a key. He gave me a spare, which I keep here in case his is lost."

"When did you realise that something was wrong?"

"I made us lunch and waited for him to return. When he didn't, I initially thought that perhaps the writing was going well and he wanted to press on with it while he was in the mood, as he has done occasionally, but when it started to get dark, I began to become uneasy and so I took the spare key and set out to find him.

"When I reached the hut, the door was locked and inside it looked as if nothing had been touched; certainly nothing to suggest that he had been interrupted while working. After having a good look around the area near to the hut, I hoped that perhaps he had returned by a different route from the one that I had taken and that he would be waiting back at home, but of course he wasn't.

"That's when I rang the police, and they came and took details and had a look around, here and in the woods. That's when they said an appeal to the public might help, and they took a photo to use for publicity."

"Has he ever gone missing before like this?"

"Just once, when a friend called to see him unexpectedly at the hut, knowing that he would most likely be there, and they ended up going for a walk and lunch at a pub, not returning until a lot later than normal. That was why I wasn't overly concerned when he didn't come back at his usual time, until the light began to fade, and then I felt sure that something was wrong."

"What do you think has happened?"

"In my head I've been coming up with all sorts of possible explanations, the idea that he has suffered memory loss and is wandering around lost somewhere, or maybe he has decided to leave his old life behind. It may be my way of trying not to think about a different sort of explanation."

"Did he show any signs of being unhappy with his current life?"

"No, not at all; just the opposite. He was enjoying the freedom of being retired, while keeping his mind ticking over with his writing."

"What sort of books does he write?"

"He likes to challenge himself with new subjects, to study something and write about it in a way that hasn't been published before." She pointed to a bookcase at the back of the room. "Those are some of his books in there."

Spike walked over to the shelves and looked along the spines of different editions bearing the author's name. There was a book on bridges of the world and their various types of construction, another on the effect of the moon on our weather patterns, and a book of a hundred unusual knots. "I thought they might have been about English Literature, given that he taught it at school."

"That would be like you writing a book on journalism," suggested Mrs Fellows. "After a lifetime of teaching, he wanted to leave that world behind."

"Was he popular with his pupils?"

"Are schoolmasters ever that popular? He got on with them well enough, but going to school is what you have to do when you aren't free to enjoy yourself. I think there's always an element of reluctance, even resentment, when you are compelled to do something, as a pupil and as a teacher earning a living. You hear people say that they had a favourite teacher when they were growing up, but I think they are letting the intervening years soften the edges of the picture in their head of what it was really like. I believe that both pupils and teachers are glad when the bell rings to restore their freedom."

"I take it from that, you didn't enjoy your schooldays?"

"My parents were both teachers, so the school holidays were like an extension of term time, which makes it even more strange that I married a schoolteacher, some people work to live and others live to work. Geoffrey is definitely in the former category."

As Spike was leaving, he asked if Mrs Fellows had a different photo from the one used in the *Evening Post*, to give his story a fresh look. As she was taking a different image out of a frame on a display cabinet, Spike wondered whether he could also borrow the key for the hut, to see for himself the place where her husband worked, if the police had returned it.

She looked a little surprised, but said: "Yes, of course," being keen to co-operate as fully as possible with any efforts to trace her missing spouse.

"I'll make sure that you get them both back," Spike assured her, as she gave him an A4-sized photo of her husband alongside her and another woman beneath a sunshade with the sea behind them, on a foreign holiday together. She also handed him a bronze Yale key attached by a keyring to a silver metal key fob.

After he had parked in the main street in front of the *Bartown Chronicle* office, Spike crossed the road to a small shop offering shoe repair and key cutting services. He waited while the assistant placed it in the jaws of a small vice, turned a wheel that made a grinding sound, and after tidying a couple of rough edges with a file, put the original and the copy on the counter.

As the assistant put the old key back on the ring that had come with it, he said: "Popular key fob these." Spike raised his eyebrows in puzzlement. "That's two days running someone's come in with one of them." Spike glanced at the fob as he paid for the copy, and then slipped them both in his pocket.

As he crossed back over the road, Carl was also returning to the office, a striped blue-and-white bakery bag clutched in his hand, and he followed him up the stone steps and through to the reporters' room. Carl laid his coat across the far side of his desk, in the characteristic manner, and sparked the gas fire into action beside his desk. He unwrapped some sandwiches and took a bite, chewing enthusiastically.

"Tom's out at a meeting with the police chief. How was your visit to the headmaster's office? Did you get the cane or did he give you a gold star?"

"I don't think I got anything from him, apart from making him bristle when I suggested it could be an inside job."

Carl rubbed his hands in front of the fire. "You think someone at the college might have something to do with it? Maybe your missing man is hiding in one of the quadrangles."

"You've been there before, have you?"

"I've had the pleasure of Mr Urquhart's company, yes. It's all a bit jolly hockey sticks for my liking up there. Tuck shop and mater and pater, with eye-wateringly high school fees to be paid."

Sitting at his desk, Spike let his chair rock back onto its rear legs and stretched his arms behind his head to get comfortable. With Carl sober, it seemed like a good time to ask him about the man with no name "I was going to ask your opinion about something." He watched Carl take another big bite of his sandwich. "If someone said to you that they were going to kill someone, would you take them seriously?"

Carl chewed and thought for a moment. "That depends on who they had in mind. I can think of a couple of people I wouldn't mind seeing the back of. I don't exactly wish them dead, but I might just count to ten before telling someone not to do it. Why d'you ask? Has someone been going round issuing death threats?"

"Just some bloke in a pub who was the worst for drink. I didn't think anything of it at the time, but he said it was going to be his teacher, and now a teacher has gone missing, it's made me wonder."

"Do you know who he is?"

"I don't know his name, but I've got a phone number for him. He made me write it down in my notebook. Said I'd be needing it."

"There's your answer, then. Ring him up and have it out with him. No point in agonising over it when you can confront him with it. 'A problem deferred is a problem doubled.' Just don't agree to meet him on some remote cliff top beauty spot on the edge of a sheer drop because he says he wants to admire the lovely view."

There was a noise from the other end of the office, and both looked up quickly to see Harry Dixon standing in the doorway of Tom's office.

"Afternoon, gents. I was just looking through some of the old bound copies of the paper, to see whether our missing man had ever had a mention. I couldn't help overhearing what you said about a threat to kill a teacher. I'd be interested in hearing what he has to say when you get in touch."

Spike wanted to tell him how rude it was to eavesdrop people's conversations, but Harry had given himself an excuse to be hidden around the corner. He'd only say it was accidental if he were challenged. But that didn't change the fact that Harry now knew about the chief suspect. Spike also wanted to confront him about how there had been nothing for him on police calls the previous morning, but he was forming the impression that the less he said to Harry Dixon the better. Watching Carl eating was making him hungry, so he said: "I'm going to grab a bite to eat." He hoped Carl would make his feelings known while he went a couple of doors down the road to the bakery shop.

When he came back a few minutes later, bag in hand, he heard the whistle of the kettle in the office kitchen along the hall, where Carl was making himself a brew. As Spike opened the door to the reporters' room, Harry was standing over his desk looking at something on it. It was then that Spike realised in his haste to leave he had left his notebook beside his typewriter, ready to write up the interviews from this morning. He hadn't opened it, but now it lay open on the surface.

Harry had given a little jump as the door had opened, and moved back to his own desk nearby. Spike walked up to his desk and looked at the notebook, which was open at a place a few pages back from the most recent entry, where he had written a phone number. Next to the number Spike had put 'The Man with No Name'.

He gave Harry a glare. "I thought eavesdropping was bad enough, but cribbing from another person's notebook while they're out of the room is even worse."

If Harry felt uncomfortable about being caught, he didn't show it. He even smiled slightly. "Don't tell me you wouldn't have done the same."

"No, I wouldn't. And I'd be ashamed at being caught."

"That's the difference between us then. We do what we have to do in this game, and let other people decide afterwards whether it's wrong or right. Those who bleat about it are the ones standing on the sidelines watching; they haven't got the guts to do anything themselves. If you want to get on, you'll learn that. In my world, the ends always justify the means."

Spike was wondering how he'd ended up on the receiving end of a lecture when Carl returned carrying two mugs of coffee. He put one on his desk and carried the other across to Harry. "The kettle's just boiled," he said to Spike, seeing him back. "Harry suggested a cuppa, so I offered to make him one."

Spike thought how convenient that must have been for him, but he said nothing. Instead, he took his lunch and his notebook and headed outside, saying he needed some fresh air.

There was a park just a couple of streets away from the office, and Spike made his way there, finding a spare bench to sit in the sunshine. It was April, a time when the sun could have warmth for the first time in the year, but a sharp wind could still cut through to the bone. Fortunately, it was a calm day, and the daffodils shone like ornamental lights nodding gently above the flowerbeds. A robin came down as he was eating his lunch, hopping along the path, and begged a few fragments torn from the crust before vanishing in a blur of wing beats.

Spike shook the crumbs out on the floor and then scrunched up the striped blue-and-white paper bag when he had finished. He decided to leave writing up the quotes from that morning and to follow up what he had learnt from them. He put his hand in his pocket and found the key to the hut. He looked at the silver fob, which seemed to be in the shape of a country, perhaps South America, being wider at the top and then tailing away to a point at the bottom, smooth along the 'eastern' edge but ruffled along the 'western' coast.

It was only when Spike looked closely at the smooth curved line running from top to bottom along just the left-hand edge that he realised he was looking at it from the wrong side. He turned it over and he could see that it was shaped like half a heart, the right-hand half, with the word 'Hers' inscribed on it in italics. It seemed to Spike like a good time to go for a walk in the woods.

Chapter 7

Spike followed the directions given to him by Mrs Fellows, in the direction of the River Bar, which gave the town its name, stopping in a small lay-by on a quiet, tree-lined road. As he cut the engine, he was aware of how quiet it was, out of earshot of any major highways, with just the birdsong to break the silence.

He stepped out of the car and closed the door gently, not wanting to disturb the peace, turning the key in the lock of the car door, though he felt as if it was hardly necessary, given that he was very much alone.

A little way back from the lay-by he found a path through the trees and was soon scrunching his way along it, twigs and bits of branch snapping under his feet. In the gaps between the trees there were nettles and brambles here and there, along with a few dock leaves and ferns, providing some ground cover, but the wood was so dense that it evidently didn't allow enough light to reach the forest floor to allow much vegetation to thrive.

He was just thinking that maybe he had taken a wrong turn when he saw the slatted wooden side of what looked like a large shed. It was much like the sort you would find in someone's back garden, only bigger and with a slanting roof, windows on two sides and a wooden awning over the front door. The door had a lock fitted, and Spike took out the copy of the key he'd had made, to check that it worked. It slipped in smoothly and he was able to push the door inwards and step inside.

There was a deep stillness about the interior after the movement of the trees outside. A desk and hard chair occupied the main space at the far end of the room, but there were portable shelving units on the sides and a heater with a gas cylinder close by. At the far end was an old armchair, perhaps for when he needed a more comfortable seat to ponder his next move with his writing, or even to take a short nap. It all looked very functional, as if everything had been arranged not to be distracting, with no ornaments or keepsakes to catch the eye and derail the train of thought.

Spike looked at the items on the shelves, the writing materials, a dictionary and thesaurus, a stapler and some paperclips. On the bottom shelf was an old cardboard box, and looking inside it, Spike could see various bits of rope of different thicknesses, each with a different type of knot tied in the end. There also a battery-powered desk lamp, probably for those times when the creative juices had been flowing and he had outstayed the best of the daylight, as his wife had said he occasionally did, since there was no lighting other than daylight through the windows.

Although it had probably been in place for quite a number of years, the shed still had that distinctive smell of wood that has been cut and treated, in the same way as a new car keeps its smell for several years after it has left the showroom. Spike looked up into the roof, where a few cobwebs indicated that other occupants had also found the place to their liking and been busy with their own silent creativity, unnoticed by the man working diligently below.

'Where was he now?' wondered Spike, the thought occurring to him that Geoffrey Fellows could walk in now and want to know who this stranger was on his property. But he had the key to prove his permission to be there and, besides, it would be worth the awkwardness of the moment to get the story of his return all to himself.

Thinking of the key reminded him of his promise to return it, and now that he knew that his copy worked, he could do so confidently. He might not need it. There was nothing here to see. But he had learnt in the past that it paid to keep all potential avenues open until more details emerged. He would, of course, have to be more careful if he did return, perhaps best not in daylight, since having a copy of the key might lead him to having a bit of explaining to do.

Mrs Fellows was in her front garden when he called to return the key, on her knees with a trowel and gloves. She asked if he had found the hut from her directions, and invited him in, but he said he needed to make a call to someone so he wouldn't stay. He asked her if she had heard anything new, but he could tell from her demeanour that she was still waiting, and hoping. "When I heard your car pulling into the drive, I could hear my heart racing. It's the same when the phone rings, so I come out here to distract myself."

Spike wanted to say something to give her hope. He found himself making a promise, though he hadn't planned it. "I'll find him for you," he said, shocking himself with what he was saying. "I'll keep looking until I do."

He handed her the key that he had borrowed. "I like the fob," he told her. "I haven't seen one like that before."

"A friend of ours, Susan, made it for us. She makes jewellery for a living. Geoffrey asked her to do it. He has the other half with his key on it." She looked down at it in her hand for a moment, thinking, and then took the key off and held out the fob to give it back to him. "Keep it," she said. "You can give it back to me when you've found Geoffrey."

He wanted to tell her that he hoped she got some good news soon, but they seemed like empty words when he formed them in his head just prior to saying them, so he held them back and just smiled in what he hoped was a sympathetic way. "The garden looks nice," he said instead.

"It keeps me busy. There's always lots to do out here at this time of year. It makes me think about something else."

On the way back into town he stopped beside a phone box and opened his notebook at the page showing the number for the man at the pub. He thought about what he was going to say as he found a coin in his pocket, and then tapped it distractedly on the metal shelf as he waited for the call to connect.

A few seconds went by with no ringing at the other end, just silence, and then a long 'Bleeeeep!' of the disconnected tone. He tried again, thinking that he may have dialed the wrong number, or turned the disc with his forefinger in the holes a little too quickly, but got the same result.

———

Perhaps it was the phone, he hoped, though there had been a dialing tone when he had replaced the receiver on the cradle and picked it up again, putting it to his ear. Public phone boxes were always getting vandalised, having matchsticks or chewing gum jammed in the coin slots or the receiver tampered with, but it seemed to be okay.

When he tried another box a little further along the road and got the same result, he knew that he'd been given a wrong number. It felt like a door had been slammed in his face. He could still hear the man's voice saying: "Write down my phone number. You'll need it when it happens."

That evening he came in to the office to see whether the new edition of the *Bartown Chronicle* had been delivered. On the floor inside the door, he found the bundles of copies to be sold over the counter, and finding a pair of scissors on the receptionists' desk he cut the string holding one of the bundles together and took the delivery address print-out off the top of the pile.

He took out two copies and tucked them under his arm, making his way back out onto the now-quiet main street in the fading light. Back at home he opened one of the papers, spreading its broadsheet form on a table to flick through the pages, looking mainly at the stories that he had written, but also glancing at those of his colleagues. He was pleased with the article on the man in court, accompanied by Kat's photo of his escape into his car from the man's dogs, and the piece on Sapphire, with Kat's photo alongside. He folded the paper and left it there, taking the unopened one with him in his car, back to the big house with the tall columns outside the front door, his car's suspension complaining again as he bumped the wheels up the tall kerb onto the driveway.

As he introduced himself on the doorbell intercom, he said: "I've brought you a copy of tomorrow's paper, to show you the article." The buzzer signaled his invitation to come inside.

"Do you provide this service for everyone you interview?" asked Sapphire, allowing herself a smile this time. "That must take up a lot of your time."

Spike knew she wanted confirmation that it was a special favour. "I just thought you might like to see it, ahead of all the rush in demand for your services that I'm sure will follow."

"There wasn't an ulterior motive for coming to see me?" she asked. What was it about her that made him think she could read his mind? 'Best to be honest,' she had said last time. "There was a favour I wanted to ask, but have a look at the article first."

He handed her the paper and told her the page number as she flicked through, putting on a pair of glasses that balanced close to the end of her nose to read his words.

"Very good," she said eventually. "I'm not sure about the headline: 'Mind your own business', but otherwise it reads very well."

"I don't write the headlines," Spike said to her in his defence, though even as he said it, he was aware that it sounded lame. He felt a sense of relief. There had been times when readers had disliked what he had written about them, taking issue with things that he knew they had said but now regretted sharing with him, and so claimed inaccuracy. Once someone had told him that one of the details in his report had been said in confidence, though he knew that it hadn't. It had made him wonder why anyone would tell a reporter writing in a notebook something that they didn't want others to know, but they had.

She folded the paper. "What was the favour you were going to ask?"

He pointed to the front of the paper. "That story about the missing teacher. I'm trying to find out what has happened. After I spoke to you in the pub, I was approached by a man who told me he was going to kill a teacher. I didn't take him seriously at the time, but he made me write down his phone number. I've tried to ring it, but just got a wrong number tone. It's left me facing a bit of a dead end."

She paused for a moment, looking closely at him in a way that made him feel uncomfortable. He had to look away, as if not turning away would have harmed his eyes.

"Why do you want to know?" she said eventually.

"I want to find out the truth about what happened."

"No, why do you *really* want to know?"

Spike felt a twinge of conscience as he examined more deeply his motives for knowing. "I've got a rival in the office. I suppose I want to find out before he does."

"You want to be first with the news, but when it's printed, everybody knows, so you have to find something else new, and then something else, to keep being first, like a dog chasing its tail."

He felt slightly ashamed. "Show me your notebook," she said. Spike took the pad out of his pocket and opened it at the right page. "Take out the 1 in the middle and it will work."

Spike was amazed. "Really? How do you know that?"

"It begins with a 3, so it's a lower Bartown number, but they have only five digits, whereas this has six. You've written the number down wrongly. Instead of a double 1 in the middle it should have only a single 1." Spike hadn't considered trying other permutations. He had just assumed that he had been given a wrong number.

"It's an easy mistake to make," she said. "Anybody could make it, just as anybody could work out what was wrong with it."

"I couldn't see it," he said.

"You only think you couldn't. You give up too easily, and don't believe in yourself enough to work things out. If you'd thought about it, you'd have known."

He decided to chance his arm with a more ambitious question. "Will this number lead me to the missing man?"

She got up, aware that he had been emboldened by his success. "Ring the number first and find out what the person who answers has to say, then you can take it from there."

40

Sapphire thanked him again for the paper, and as he got into his car, he glanced up at the window at her. Perhaps she was right. Perhaps he needed to have more faith in himself.

Chapter 8

There were two people waiting for Spike outside his home the next morning when he walked up the drive towards his car in the road outside. One was the now-familiar face of the taxi driver, and the other was a woman, presumably the taxi driver's wife. She was a good deal larger than he was, full faced and with a fuller figure. The sight of them standing side by side waiting for him put Spike in mind of the children's nursery rhyme about Jack Sprat, who could eat no fat, and his wife who could eat no lean, but between them both they licked the platter clean. He almost wanted to call him Jack as he approached, and ask him if he and Joan had a cat that got the bones after they had dined, but he thought better of it.

"Still here, then?" the taxi driver began, stepping between Spike and his car.

"Certainly looks like it," Spike told him.

"Not taken my advice?" the man asked, trying to sound menacing.

"Are you going to let me get to my car or am I going to have to call the police and get them to remove you?"

"Them's not going to help you. You don't belong 'ere. I'll tell 'em you assaulted me, and I've got a witness. Two on to one, so it'd be our word 'gainst yours. You're all alone, mate, best you realise that."

Spike waited for the triumphant smirk to hang on the taxi driver's face for a couple of seconds before he took the tape machine out of his top pocket and pressed the rewind button, followed by 'Play'.

'You don't belong 'ere. I'll tell 'em you assaulted me, and I've got a witness,' the voice said. The smirk melted away.

"Are you going to move or do I need to take this to the police and let them hear it?" Spike brushed past the taxi driver, got in his car and drove away, but he knew that the running battle wouldn't end there and next time there would be worse to come.

The office diary was an A4 book with a hard black cover in which were written the year's various events, from carnival parades and agricultural shows to council meetings and the fringe festival, along with details of staff holidays. Next to each entry was a set of initials indicating which person had been allocated what job.

As Spike looked down at the open ledger, on the desk next to the window in the reporters' room, he saw the letters 'SP' next to an entry under today's date that read: 'Golden Wedding couple'. He went into Tom's office to find out more.

Tom consulted a letter on his desk, the rich aroma of pipe smoke drifting from the ashtray at his elbow. "Bob and Barbara Chivers," he told Spike. "We've had a note from their daughter asking if we would like to meet them and put something in the paper. If you give them a ring and drop in there this morning you can find out what it's like to have been married for fifty years." He handed Spike the letter. "Get Kat to come with you and get a pic of them cutting the cake."

He had a copy of the new edition of the *Bartown Chronicle* on his desk, with the front-page story of the missing man visible. "I've had a meeting with the chief inspector about favouring our friend with their news items. I've given them my number as a point of contact for anything of interest from now on, to short cut the police front desk, so we'll see how that works out. I'll feed you anything that I think is worth a story."

Spike pulled up in the street outside Kat's house, where she lived with her mother. The metal gate sounded a familiar note as he pushed it open and knocked on the door. He admired the circle of crocuses poking up through the grass beneath a small tree in the front garden while he waited for the door to be answered. Kat's mother had her sleeves rolled up as if she was busy with some household task, and a few seconds later Kat was behind her, coat on and camera case over her shoulder.

"Thought I'd save you the petrol, as I was coming past your place," said Spike.

"What do we know about the couple? Anything unusual that might make a different picture?"

"Not at first glance. Something about a special brooch to mark the occasion, but I think the usual cake shot will suffice. Not much chance to flex your creative muscles on this one. Talking about flexing your muscles, how's the karate going?"

"Really well. I'm enjoying it."

"I thought you might say you'd given it the chop."

She gave him a withering look. "I think you need a holiday. You're even sounding like one of your stories now."

As they turned into the street where the couple lived, Spike took the letter out of his pocket and rested it on the dashboard. The address was given as number forty-five, and as they counted down the house numbers, he could see some bunting and balloons in a front garden up ahead.

"I'm no expert, but I'd say that may be our destination up there," he said. Two golden balloons in the shape of the number fifty swayed on strings from the gate, and a couple of visitors were already walking down the path towards the house.

Kat and Spike followed them, Kat pausing to take a close-up photo of a perfect blood-red camellia flower glowing in the sun on a bush in the front garden as they passed. It was something that separated her from other photographers that Spike had worked alongside. Many restricted their picture taking to the job in hand, some not even getting their camera out of their bag until it was needed, but she always had one around her neck ready to use and was constantly looking about for anything of interest to photograph.

Spike had asked her once about it and she had said that because there were thirty-six shots on a roll of film, often a lot of frames didn't get used, a dozen images being plenty for most staged photo jobs. So rather than waste the other frames, she used them for her portfolio, taking anything that caught her eye.

They were invited in by the writer of the note to a gathering of friends and relatives, seated in various armchairs and dining chairs placed around the living room. Adjoining it was a dining room leading to a set of French windows and a table laden with food for a buffet, along with a large iced cake.

As Kat attached a flashgun to her camera, Spike was introduced to the couple and got a few details. They had donned their best clothes for the occasion, and had with them some of their various children and grandchildren, which they listed for Spike's benefit. When he'd asked them about how they met and what their secret was for a happy marriage, hoping in vain that they would come up with something more original than 'Give and take', he was shown a commemorate brooch that their daughter had commissioned for the occasion. It had photos of them both within a heart shape with a '5' and a '0' attached at its base.

Spike was introduced to the lady who had made it, and he knew as soon as he saw her that her face was familiar. "This is Susan," said the couple's daughter, and in a moment Spike was transported to the front room of Mrs Fellows' home, and the picture that she had leant him of herself and her husband on holiday.

"Susan makes jewellery," he was told. "Isn't it lovely?"

"It is, yes," agreed Spike. He turned to the woman beside him. "Would you be willing to let us do a story about your work for the paper?"

The maker of the brooch looked surprised, but before she had been given a chance to be modest and demur, her hosts said that would be lovely and cajoled her into it.

Spike wrote down her phone number, carefully this time, while Kat arranged the couple around the cake, sharing the knife provided for the expected ritual with their hands both making the cut amid flashes from the camera.

Politely turning down offers of food and drinks on the grounds of a busy work schedule, the two visitors left the couple to their friends and family, dodging the balloons on the gate once more as they made their way back to the car.

"That wasn't too painful," said Spike. "I've been at ones that become a struggle to get away. I've practically been force fed sponge cake and scones before I've been allowed to leave."

"I thought it was nice," said Kat. "The time will come when there aren't any Golden Weddings any more, which will be sad."

Spike dropped her back at her house and she said she'd send the photos through. He was already thinking about what he was going to do next, and a red phone box at the end of the road provided the opportunity. Inside, he curled the dial round in accordance with the five numbers, watching it tick back around to where it had started, and seconds later heard a ringing tone. She had been right about the five digits, but was it the right number?

As Spike was beginning to think that no one would answer, the phone clicked into life and a man's voice said: "Hello?"

"I don't know whether you remember me, but I think we spoke outside the Horse & Barge pub a few days ago? I wrote your number down in my n…"

"I wondered when I'd be hearing from you," said the voice at the other end. She had been right about the number as well.

"Have you seen the story about the missing teacher in the papers?"

"Of course."

"It made me think of what you'd said to me."

There was a pause for a moment, just silence on the other end of the line. Then the man said: "I was drunk. We all say things we regret when we've been drinking."

Spike thought he didn't sound very convincing. In his experience, when someone is innocent, they are open and expansive, happy to talk at length to show that they aren't to blame. "So, it's just a coincidence about the teacher?" More silence at the other end of the line. "Do you still go to the Horse & Barge sometimes?" asked Spike.

"Occasionally."

"Can we meet up?"

"What for?"

"Just to clear the air. Put my mind at rest." He half expected a refusal, but it seemed as though his non-threatening tone had worked.

"What time?"

"How about in an hour?"

"Okay."

"On the same bench outside."

"Right."

"I'll see you there."

"Cheers."

The man with no name hadn't sounded very enthusiastic about meeting again, and there was a strong possibility that he wouldn't turn up and had just said yes to get rid of his caller, but if he did, at least Spike felt reasonably safe in a public place in daylight. And he hadn't mentioned being contacted by Harry Dixon, so it could be that the number mistake would work in Spike's favour. There was just time to write the Golden Wedding story in his notebook ahead of his rendezvous, so he curled up in the front seat of his car and put together the piece in longhand, ready to be typed out when he returned to the office.

It was a habit that he had always found satisfying, benefiting from the solitude without the inevitable interruptions to his thought process from having people around him. It made him think of Geoffrey Fellows and his writing hut. He could picture him there, filling pages while seated at his desk, oblivious to the rest of the world. There was no doubt that writing offered an escape to a dreamlike state where the passage of time didn't seem to exist.

At school once, in a crowded classroom, he had lost himself so completely in a story that he had been writing that he had drifted outside of his surroundings entirely, and felt a deep sense of shock when he had suddenly become aware again of his location, as if he had been dropped back into his seat from the sky with a bump.

What had made the moment even more surprising was that he had been sitting an exam at the time, and felt a moment of intense panic as he returned from his 'dream', glancing quickly at his wristwatch on the desk beside him to check that he hadn't almost run out of time.

Perhaps that was something the man with no name had experienced, too, having been good at writing, that almost spiritual moment of profound reverie when all connection with reality is lost for a short time through creativity, as you travel to another time and place. But for now, he needed to answer a more urgent question, and that was whether his acquaintance was linked to the disappearance of Geoffrey Fellows.

It was quieter this time in the Horse & Barge, and without the distraction of waiting customers, Sapphire saw him as he walked through the door. She smiled in greeting. "You're becoming a regular," she said. "We'll be keeping a tankard with your name on it behind the bar next."

"I thought maybe a comfy stool with my initials on the seat in gold lettering would suffice. A bit more classy."

"What can I get you?" Spike ordered a drink and explained the reason for his visit. "You got through on that number, then?" she asked.

"I never doubted that I would." He took a sip of his beer. "If you get a moment, could you have a glance out of the door at us and see whether you recognise him?" he asked.

"Give him the once over?"

"In a manner of speaking. I'm trying to work out whether he's a fantasist or the real deal. He says it was just the drink talking, but I'm not so sure."

"There is a way of finding out."

Spike paused, stopping his drink abruptly on its way towards his open mouth. "There is?"

"You could ask him what school he attended. If it wasn't Bartown College, that would rule him out."

Once again Spike found himself wondering why he hadn't thought of her suggestion himself. She had been right about that as well, he needed to start thinking things through for himself, instead of relying on others to provide solutions to his problems.

Another customer needed to be served, so Spike took his drink outside to wait for his acquaintance. The sun was warm when it peeked from behind the clouds, but it was more often than not hidden from view, and with nothing to occupy himself he soon began to feel cold. He looked at his watch and saw that it was well past the hour that he'd arranged on the phone. He was thinking that he had wasted his time when Sapphire appeared beside him.

"Been stood up?"

"It looks a bit that way."

"Maybe he's watching you from a discreet distance, deciding whether he can trust you, looking to see whether you've brought someone with you."

She had just finished speaking when a voice behind her said: "Hello!" They both turned to see the man with no name walking towards them. This time there was no wobble to his gait and no unnervingly long and silent smile. Sapphire offered to take his order and bring his drink out to him.

The man sat in the same place as he had before, but with a more focused look. "Thanks for coming," Spike said.

"Sorry I'm a bit late. I wanted to check it wasn't a set-up."

"I wouldn't do that," Spike reassured him. "Journalists always protect the people who give them tip-offs."

"You can't trust nobody these days."

"Tell me about it. You can see why I rang, though?"

"Yeah, 'course."

"But I'm worrying unnecessarily?"

"I haven't killed anyone, if that's what you mean."

"Or abducted them?"

"Seems more like murder to me."

Spike was surprised. "Why d'you say that?"

Now it was the newcomer's turn to look surprised. "On account of the shoe."

Sapphire returned with his drink and took his money, but Spike barely noticed her. "The shoe?"

"They've found his shoe. I heard it on the local radio when I was listening to it on the way here. It was in the grass beside a lay-by on the main road."

Spike struggled to compute the news. "It's definitely his?"

"That's what they said."

He knew he had to be elsewhere, to find out what had happened and to follow up this new development. He made his apologies and headed for his car. It was only when he was driving back to the office that he suddenly remembered he hadn't asked about the man's school, and still didn't know his name. But he had seemed a lot less unnerving than when he had been drunk, to the point where Spike had almost discounted him from his suspicions.

Chapter 9

The reporters' room was empty when Spike pushed open the door, but he could hear the sound of typing from the office behind. He put his head inside the back room and found Tom tapping out a story.

"I hear there's been a development in the missing teacher story," he said to his editor.

"What's that?"

Spike couldn't disguise the surprise in his voice. "The shoe!"

"Shoe? What shoe?"

"They've found a shoe belonging to him… or so I was told. Don't tell me it's not true."

"There was nothing about that on police calls," Tom told him. "I spoke to them only about half an hour ago."

Spike had that slow feeling of betrayal that comes from trusting someone too much. He had been so keen to find out more, he hadn't stopped to think about the authenticity of his source.

"Who told you?" asked Tom.

The question served only to add to Spike's sense of having been duped. He could hear the honest answer sounding in his head, that of: 'Just some bloke I met in a pub; I don't know his name,' but he couldn't bring himself to say it. Instead, he said: "Someone I thought was reliable, but maybe he isn't."

A thought occurred to him. "Have you still got that radio in the office?"

Tom opened a drawer of his desk and took out a hand-sized plastic set with a telescopic aerial and earphones, passing them to Spike. "He said he heard it on the radio," Spike told him in explanation, taking the device through to his chair in the reporters' room.

When it was almost time for the news bulletin, on the hour, he tuned it in and found the local radio station's wavelength. He listened to a story about the county council budget cuts and the threatened strike by bus drivers in the north of the region, but heard nothing to make him feel less gullible about being taken in by the man outside the pub.

He tried ringing the number in his notebook, chewing on the end of his pen as he waited but, as he'd suspected, there was no answer. He wouldn't have got back home yet, unless he had but wasn't answering.

While he was replacing the receiver, the door swung open and Carl appeared. He didn't even remove his coat before turning on the fire next to his desk in his customary manner, rubbing his hands together as he did so.

"Bloody hell! Is it just me or is it freezing in here?" he asked. "It's as cold as a husky's nose. I thought it was supposed to be spring." He took a cigarette out of a box in his pocket and lit the end from the front of the gas fire.

Spike asked him what he'd been up to as he watched the bricks of the fire gradually take on an orange glow. "I've been to see a girl who hasn't stopped sneezing for two years. She's been told she'll make the Guinness Book of Records if she isn't cured in the next six months. She's been signed up to do an advert for a paper tissue brand. I've never said: 'Bless you!' so many times in an interview before. How was your Golden Wedding?"

"Enough cake to feed an army, but no unusual secrets for a happy married life. Not like the last one I did, when the bloke said: 'Infidelity.'"

"Have you tracked down your friendly murder suspect yet?" Carl asked.

"Yes, but he claims it was the drink talking, though he didn't help himself by telling me something that no one else seems to know about it. I was writing him off, but now I'm not so sure." Spike nodded towards the empty chair in front of him. "And with no sign of our friend from the *Evening Post* today, I think there's something brewing."

When copies of the paper were brought through from the front office with the internal post on the van and handed round, Spike had a feeling of misgiving even before he had opened his copy.

'Missing man shoe shock find,' read the headline. 'Police believe he has come to harm.'

The exclusive story by Harry Dixon began: 'A shoe belonging to missing teacher Geoffrey Fellows has been found in woods close to his home. The dramatic development has prompted police to scale up efforts to find him amid fears that he has come to harm.

'His distraught wife confirmed the shoe as one of his, and appealed for anyone who has seen him to come forward. It was discovered during a fingertip search by officers at woodland in Bartown owned by the couple, in vegetation close to a lay-by on an adjoining road. The retired college teacher has a writing hut on the land, from which he has composed a series of books.

'Chief Inspector James Parish said: "We need to find Mr Fellows as a matter of urgency. In response to the discovery of an item of his clothing, the investigation into his disappearance has been escalated, with more resources and manpower being diverted into finding him. We would like to hear from anyone who thinks they may have seen a man answering his description in the area in the past five days. While we hope fervently that he can be reunited with his family safe and well, this latest development raises concerns that he may be being held somewhere against his will or have come to harm."'

Spike looked at the empty desk in front of him. Some people were more of a problem when they weren't around than when they were, because it meant they were up to something.

Tom walked through from his office, newspaper in hand. "We seem to be the last to hear about anything around here. We're playing catch-up all the time. See if you can find out something about what's been going on, even if you have to buy them a few drinks to loosen their tongues. Someone out there knows something, and we could do with getting to them before the police. Have a nose around the houses close to this bit of land that they own and see if anyone knows anything."

Spike was sure that there was one resident who did know something, and he could be back home by now. When he spotted a phone box close to where the streets of houses gave way to open fields, he pulled over and dialed the number.

The phone rang several times before it was answered. The voice on the other end was the familiar one of the man with no name. He sounded a bit disappointed, as if he had been expecting someone else to call. "Oh, it's you."

"Sorry to bother you again, only there are a couple of things I was going to ask but I didn't get round to it, with leaving suddenly. Can I call in and see you?"

There was a pause that told Spike how reluctant the man on the other end was to allow him any closer. "It's not a good time. I've got someone coming round."

Spike was ready for the attempt to fob him off. "It wouldn't take long. I'm in the area already. Just a couple of quick questions and then I'll leave you to it."

This time the pause was in Spike's favour. He could sense that the man had run out of excuses to keep him away. "If it's quick."

"I can be there in a moment. I just need the address."

Spike scribbled the address in his notebook as it was dictated to him, the phone's receiver crooked between his shoulder blade and his ear. There was always a rush of pride and a sense of accomplishment with every small victory that opened a new avenue.

The ground-floor flat was very sparsely furnished. An armchair facing a TV set, a small dining table and, through an open door, a bed and a side table seemed to be about the extent of the household possessions, with one exception. Behind the door in the living room, in the opposite corner from the TV, was an exercise machine. Hanging above the workout bench were a series of handles connected by thick wires to pulleys that operated the stack of weights. It looked to Spike like some kind of torture equipment, the sort that you might find in a tourist attraction dungeon.

His host noticed Spike peering at it as he walked in. "I like to keep fit," said the man. He sat on the bench, leaving Spike the only armchair.

"I meant to ask you your name earlier," Spike said, perching on the front of the chair's cushion.

"I'd rather not say. The less you know about me the better, I reckon."

"But if you've done nothing wrong, you've got nothing to worry about."

"That's not how things work. I wouldn't be the first person to get collared for something he didn't do."

"What about naming the school that you went to? That would put you in the clear."

The man thought for a moment, pursing his lips as he considered the implications of acceding to Spike's request.

"Saint Theresa's," he said, watching for Spike's reaction, but his head was down, writing in his notebook.

"How are you spelling that? I can never remember."

"With an 'h'."

"Yes, of course. And I just wanted to check that you said you heard about the shoe on the radio. It's just that I listened to the radio when I got back to the office and the news didn't mention it."

"It must have been in the paper. I don't remember where. Or maybe someone mentioned it on the bus." He glanced at his watch. "Is there anything else, 'cause I've got someone coming?"

"Just one more thing. Does the name Harry Dixon mean anything to you?"

"Who?"

"I thought you might have had a phone call from someone with that name, but maybe not."

"Doesn't ring a bell, but then people use different names when it suits them." He got up, holding Spike to his word that he'd had only one more question, and the inference was clearly that it was time to go.

"Thanks for your time. With a bit of luck some more evidence will come to light that will put you in the clear." He looked at the man's face, but saw nothing to suggest that he was expecting good news to come his way.

Spike drove around the corner and then cut the engine, watching in his rear-view mirror the section of pavement in front of the flats. For a while nothing happened, and he had almost decided to move on when the man he had just been talking to, now wearing an overcoat, walked down his front path and away in the opposite direction, striding purposely into the distance.

When his footsteps had faded out of earshot, Spike started his car and drove in the opposite direction from the man on foot, but turned left at the end of the estate, and left again at the next main road, which took him to the road out of town that the man had been heading along. When he joined it, he was just a short distance from the lay-by beside the wood owned by Geoffrey Fellows.

He drove past, finding an entrance to a field with a farm gate that he could back his car into so that it was out of view from along the road, but with the wood still in sight. It wasn't long before the familiar figure of the man with no name appeared in the distance, walking along the road. When he reached the lay-by, he turned into the entrance to the wood and disappeared into the trees. Spike glanced at his watch. The light was beginning to fade. He shuffled further down into the driver's seat, so that he could be more comfortable, able to rest his head, but not comfortable enough to be at risk of falling asleep.

Occasionally cars went by, but they didn't stop. It was fully dark when he finally saw any movement near the lay-by. Although the person was now just a silhouette, he recognised the now-familiar gait of the man he had watched go in, walking in the opposite direction from the one that he had come from, heading back towards home.

Spike gave him long enough to get out of sight of the wood before he reached for the door handle to get out and walk back along the road. As he did so he heard the sound of a car coming, so he waited for it to pass. But unlike the others that he had seen coming along the quiet road, this one was slowing. It pulled into the lay-by and the lights were turned off. For a moment nothing happened, but then the interior light came on as the driver got out, shutting the door behind him so carefully that it didn't make a sound.

He popped the boot open and then struggled to get a large red suitcase out over the lip and on to the ground. The figure glanced around him, up and down the road, and then lowered the boot lid gently until it was closed.

Gathering the straps of the case together, the figure carried it away from the car. The weight was such that he had to lean to his left to make any headway, and every few yards he stopped to change hands. His feet almost collided with the case with every other step, but he managed to struggle down into the wood and out of sight.

Spike considered following him, but he knew that there would be even less light under the cover of the trees to see what he was walking towards. The thin moon at least provided some illumination back here on the road, so he decided to wait. Once again, he shuffled down in his seat, but this time there was no danger of him falling asleep. He could hear his heart pumping hard, tapping out a rapid beat that vibrated through him.

He was glad that he wasn't getting out just yet, giving him a chance to gather himself. He had developed a habit of trying to calm himself in stressful situations by offering mundane explanations for what he was seeing, doing the opposite of letting his imagination run away with itself. It was a game that he played with himself, but it wasn't working now. Every time he thought about what he had just seen, it sent a sense of fear through him. Whatever way he looked at it, there was no benign conclusion. He knew that whatever happened next, things were not going to end well.

It was completely dark before his wait was finally over. The moon had continued on its journey through the night sky, and what little light it had to offer to illuminate the scene was partially obscured by cloud when the man reappeared.

He still had the case, though it seemed to be hanging at an odd angle, and there was no comparison with before in terms of its weight. He carried it one-handed with ease, its contents no doubt no longer inside.

Again, he glanced up and down the empty road, before popping open the boot, lobbing the case inside and this time slamming the lid. Inside the car it was the same with the door, no longer shut gently, and even before the sound of it had left Spike's ears, the engine had been started and the car was speeding away.

The silence that followed was just as disturbing, because it said to Spike that his time of keeping out of the way was over. He pulled on the handle of the car door and was soon walking towards the entrance to the wood.

Under the covering of trees, it was as dark as he'd expected. Old leaves rustled under his shoes on the springy floor, and he had to walk slowly to avoid colliding with the trunks as he wove his way between them. The air was close and damp, heavy with the smell of vegetation. He was glad that he had been to the hut before, and so knew the way more or less, and also knew what to expect. It still seemed further than he had remembered from when it had been light, but eventually he saw the sharp outline of the roof and was aware of where he was.

He put his hand in his pocket and found the copy of the key that he had made, feeling good about having decided to have it cut. It was strange how he sometimes got an inkling about needing to do something, even though he didn't know how it would be useful, and more often than not he had found following his instincts to be the right way to go.

The key slid into the lock, and the latch yielded, allowing the door to be opened. Spike stepped inside, the room being even darker than outside. He put his hand out in front of him to feel for anything in his path as he made his way slowly towards the far wall. He remembered that there had been a lamp on the desk, and he felt his way along to where he expected it to be, not wanting to knock it over by moving too quickly. His mind struggled to picture what was in front of him when it didn't seem to conform to what was in his head, but then he felt the cold metal of the bulb and the head of the lamp, and he found the switch to turn it on.

As the battery responded, light made the area around the desk glow, and he could see that he was in familiar surroundings, though the deep pools of darkness alongside every object gave the scene a sinister feel. He let his eyes become accustomed to the light before he made his way around to look for anything that seemed to have changed since his previous visit.

He opened a cupboard, but everything looked the same, and looked around on the floor, but there was no trace of disturbance. Only a few bits of debris in the middle of the floor seemed unfamiliar, as if something had been disturbed, something that hadn't been cleaned for a while that had shed its covering of old cobwebs and dust.

He looked up above where they had fallen, but the downward-facing hood of the table lamp meant the light was poor in the roof. He picked up a bamboo cane leaning against the wall and poked it into the darkness above the beam overhead. When he expected it to pass over the beam and through to the other side, it wouldn't go. Spike poked a little harder, but still something was stopping it, though he couldn't see what.

He gave it one more poke, this time with greater force, and heard a noise that he realised was the movement of an object succumbing to the force of gravity. As soon as it did, Spike wished he hadn't given it that decisive impetus that had created sufficient inertia to send it on its way, because in the second that it began to fall, he was simultaneously aware that what was coming down was both heavy and unstoppable.

He stepped back in shock at having unwittingly freed something and at not knowing what it was, but the object didn't fall in a natural path. It jerked suddenly, being tethered at one end, and instead of falling away from him below the opposite side of the beam, it swung towards him under it with great force.

It hit him just as he ducked away, knocking him off balance and onto the floor. As he turned on the ground to look at what had collided with him, he saw the unmistakable form of a human body, still suspended from above by a rope tied around its neck.

Spike scrabbled to his feet, just out of reach of the swinging corpse, the feet rising high in the air like a child on a playground swing being pushed by an adult. It was then that he saw that the feet had only one shoe.

Chapter 10

It was only when he was outside the door of the hut that Spike was able to take a proper breath. He gasped as he leant against the wooden panels, as if he'd been running. Maybe he had. He wasn't aware of anything between the sight of the swinging shape and being back out in the wood. His body had acted of its own accord, taking control, bypassing his mind. Now it was allowing the normal order to resume, giving way to thoughts and considered responses. He needed to get away, and then he needed to think and plan what to do, but right now his head wasn't capable of such things.

He began walking, stumbling on the uneven ground, almost colliding with the tree trunks as they appeared just inches from his face. It seemed to take an age to find light in the sky ahead, but then he saw the road and his feelings of panic began to ease a little.

Inside his car he locked the door and sat for a moment, his eyes closed, but he couldn't stop the flashbacks. He listened to his heartbeat and told himself that it was slowing, that he was recovering, but every time he tried to weigh up what to do, and thought again about what he had seen, it began quickening again.

He knew that he had to resist the urge to just act. Whatever he did, it had to be a considered response, not an impulse decision. His instinct was to tell someone, the need to disseminate information was as natural to a reporter as breathing, but the crucial question was who. He considered the candidates: the police; Tom; the widow; even Sapphire. None of them seemed right, and he knew why, because he had decided already without realising it. Forming the list of options in his head had just been an attempt to sideline his intent, to avoid the prospect of what he knew he was going to do all along, playing games with himself, looking at the various options that were pointing away from him all around, knowing that he would never travel along those paths, but imagining himself walking down them just the same, to judge whether they felt right.

He started the car, taking a route he knew well, ending at a familiar front door with a welcoming light behind it. The middle-aged lady who answered the door smiled when she saw Spike. It was recognition accompanied by a certain fondness, because his presence always meant welcome work for her daughter.

"Kat's not back yet," she told him. "But if it's urgent you can find her at the sports hall. I'm sure she won't mind you going there."

Spike thanked her and made his way to the large rectangular building next to a big supermarket that was part of a retail park, and the shared extensive car park. The sports centre had a policy of allowing members of the public to observe the various activities, perhaps reasoning that watching was a gateway to joining. Spike found Kat among a dozen others, all dressed in robes tied at the waist, barefoot, practicing various combinations of kicks and punches against their sparring partners.

The class was breaking up when he caught her eye, and a look of surprise gave way to curiosity as to the reason for his visit. "Thinking of joining?" she joked, mopping her face with a towel.

Spike almost smiled. Experiencing levity again was like a tonic, almost a reminder of a former life. "It's not a social call. I need a photo of something, but I don't know how to ask."

Her face told him that he had conveyed enough of the seriousness of what lay ahead in his reply for her to realise that something important had happened. She knew him well enough to tell when there was a chill in his words. "I'll get my stuff. The camera bag's in the car. I'll see you at the entrance to the car park."

Spike led the way along the road to the edge of town and the lay-by beside the wood. He pulled up, Kat parking behind him. He got out and joined her in her car, where she was waiting, knowing that there needed to be an explanation before she got to work.

"I ought to warn you," Spike began. "This is one of those jobs that you won't be able to forget." He didn't want to frighten her, but he knew that the shock of not being forewarned would be worse. "The man who went missing... he isn't missing any more. I found him here earlier, hanging from a rope."

"You haven't told the police?"

"I needed to buy some time. I want to write the story and have a picture to go with it, then I'll go to the police."

She looked away from him. "That could get you in a whole lot of trouble. Maybe me, too."

"I know, but the alternative is to give away the chance I've got. I've been two steps behind all the way along with this story, but now I'm one step ahead. I don't want to give that up and be left with nothing."

She looked back at him. "It's that important to you, to take the risk? They might not even use a picture like that."

"At least they'll have the choice. We'll have done our bit, and whether it gets used is down to them. We'll know we couldn't have done any more, and not be left wishing we'd taken the opportunity."

She reached for the car door handle. "I'll get my gear out of the boot." When she had her camera and flash ready, they made their way into the gloom of the wood, their progress slow in the disorientating darkness that enveloped them. They could barely see each other let alone the path ahead, the sound of their footsteps being their only connection. Spike began to think he had lost his way when he noticed a glimmer of light. It was then that he realised he had left in such a rush he hadn't switched off the table lamp, nor had he locked the door behind him, which swung loosely in the breeze, as if beckoning them in like a hand.

———

Spike stopped just short of the entrance, making sure that Kat was still willing to go ahead. Then they stepped forward together and peered inside. The batteries in the lamp had waned since his previous visit, and an occasional flicker suggested that they didn't have much life left in them. There was still enough power to show the table and chair and, now motionless, the body suspended from the rope.

Kat lifted her camera to her eye and took several shots, the white light of the flash blinding them both temporarily. She then stepped slightly to one side, so that the figure was hidden by the door frame, to give the picture editor a less controversial alternative to consider.

Spike thought about going inside and switching off the light, but he reasoned that it would fade away soon enough, long before the police arrived. He closed the door, listening for the click as the latch engaged. "Come on, let's get out of here," he said, and they made their way along the tricky path to the safety of their cars.

Before they went their separate ways, Spike asked Kat if she would process the film and make the prints that evening, so that he could come and pick them up to take them to the head office, ready for the first editions of the next day's paper. He knew she had a makeshift darkroom in her mother's bathroom, and he arranged a time to call round after he had written the story in the office.

"Thanks," he said, finally, calmer now than he had been for the whole of the evening. "I wouldn't have asked if it hadn't been important."

"I know," she said. "I just hope it's worth it."

The pool of light around Spike's desk in the office from the Anglepoise lamp reminded him of the scene he had just left. But he preferred to work in enclosed areas when he was writing, blocking out any distractions by shrinking his world to a bubble.

The keys of his typewriter sounded loud in the quiet of the night, and might even have distracted him had he not become inured to their clacking sound by his years of pounding out stories. They now had a slightly soothing effect, recording his progress through the paragraphs towards the final 'ends' note to the subs at the base of the final folio.

The copytaking department kept one person on duty right through the night, and so he rang the number and read his words to her, an unfamiliar voice since it was the night shift, breaking the news that: "A body has been found in private woods close to Bartown, and it is believed to be that of the missing teacher Geoffrey Fellows.

"The discovery was made in the writing hut owned by the former Bartown College master and author, bringing to an end hopes that he would be found alive.

"Initial indications are that he may have died from hanging, but police have not ruled out that he may have been murdered and his body moved to the hut and arranged in such a way as to disguise the manner of his death.

"A full post mortem will be carried out to ascertain the cause of death and an approximate time frame to indicate whether foul play is suspected.

"The discovery brings to an end an extensive police search, which took a sinister turn when a single shoe belonging to the pensioner was found close to a lay-by at the entrance to the woods owned by Mr Fellows and his wife, Isabelle.

"The fully clothed body was found late last night, still wearing the one remaining shoe matching the one uncovered by police.

"The death has sent shockwaves through the quiet semi-rural community as local residents begin to come to terms with the news that there may be a killer on the loose in their community."

The copytaker checked the spelling of Spike's surname: "Pike with an 'i' or a 'y' in the middle?" It told him that she was impressed enough to know that a byline would be needed when the story went to press. He thanked her for her help before ringing off.

The roads were quiet now on the way to Kat's home. It was how Spike liked it. It had been raining while he had been inside, where he had been oblivious to the weather, and the words of a song came to mind about the rain washing the streets clean again.

He always felt a glow of satisfaction, like a sense of peace, after writing a news story. The job was done, the facts captured and the sentences composed. The stage was set for the readers to have their minds illuminated and their thoughts transported to where he had been, simply by reading his account of what had happened. They could stand in his shoes now, almost, and perhaps be as shocked as he had been.

A light on upstairs on the landing of Kat's mother's house reassured him that she had been busy, too. Instead of ringing the doorbell, in case his mother had retired for the night, he tapped gently on the front door. There was movement inside almost immediately, and Kat invited him inside.

Upstairs in the bathroom she had shallow tanks of liquid arranged and a box of photographic paper. Behind the door a black curtain had been used to block out any light from the landing, but now the coloured glow from the special darkroom light had been replaced with the normal one, the developer's alchemy having been accomplished.

"Have you written your story?" she asked as he peered into the trays.

"Yes, all done."

"You might have another one to write now," she told him. Spike looked at her, to see if she was joking, but there was no trace of humour in her eyes.

"Why?" he asked, genuinely puzzled.

"Take a look at this." Kat took a pair of tongs and lifted one of the sheets out of a tray. "I couldn't see what it was at first, so I did an enlargement."

She laid the wet and shiny sheet on a flat surface for Spike to get a closer look. Beyond the body and the table and the armchair was a pool of darkness in the corner of the room. The flashlight had only partially illuminated it because of the distance, and when it had, the brightness of the sudden light had prevented them from seeing for themselves what was there at the time. But now with the image enlarged and 'dodged' to lighten it, there was no mistake. There in the corner was a familiar face, that of Harry Dixon.

He was crouching out of sight, no doubt having heard them approaching, and would have stayed hidden had it not been for the flash. The look on his face was one of surprise, and that was now mirrored on the face of Spike looking down at the image of his colleague.

Spike swore gently under his breath. Kat was drying the images that he had come to collect. "I thought you'd say that."

"What the hell was he doing there?"

"He would probably have asked you the same question."

"Yes, but we weren't skulking out of slight in a corner. We were there doing our job."

"If you are planning to go to the police to tell them what you've found, I think you had better do it tonight rather than in the morning, or you may get woken up by the sound of your front door being smashed in."

Chapter 11

As Spike drove through the almost empty streets on the ten-mile journey to the *Evening Post* offices, that image of Harry Dixon's face had superseded the one of the body in the forefront of his mind. From now on he would always think of him as Flash Harry. His thoughts explored the possible explanations and probable implications of what they had found, and the best way to deal with what it meant.

He was no further forward with his theories by the time he parked in front of the towering office block where the paper was based, and went through the revolving doors to where a man in a uniform was sitting behind the reception desk.

Spike showed him his company pass and added his name to the list recording entry and exit times and car registration numbers. On previous visits there had sometimes been an exchange of comments between him and the night-shift security man, but the owner of this unfamiliar face had a taciturn demeanour, and Spike was glad of the absence of jocularity after the evening's events.

The lift hummed to the floor where the night editor was on duty, keeping staff informed of any major happenings that would need to be covered. If a local building caught fire or a late-night reveler ended up in the river and had to be rescued, he had staff on standby to get to the scene as the drama unfolded.

Spike introduced himself and saw a flicker of recognition in the face in front of him when he mentioned his name. On the desk in front of him was a folio of pages typed by the copytaker, the final one bearing his name, which had resonated with the night staffer on hearing it from its owner.

"The missing man body story?" he asked. "I've just been reading it."

"What did you think?" Feedback was always a rarity in newspaper work, so every opportunity was grasped firmly.

"It puzzled me," he said, not the reply that Spike had been expecting or hoping for. "I got a very similar story at about the same time from..." he glanced down to his desk to check the name.

"Harry Dixon?" asked Spike, finishing the man's sentence.

"Yes. I thought it was odd, because we usually make sure we don't duplicate efforts on covering stories."

Spike couldn't resist making a comment. "It's a wonder we didn't bump into one another."

The private joke didn't, of course, mean anything to the night editor, who continued with his train of thought. "It gives me a slight problem of which one to use."

Spike was ready for him. "Would a picture help make up your mind?"

That was more like it. This time there was a definite widening of the pupils of the man with the choice of stories. "A picture?"

Spike opened the envelope that he had been carrying and pulled out its contents. "Two pictures, to be precise, depending on how squeamish you think the readers are."

Spike handed them over and watched the man's head jerk back in surprise. "Bloody hell! Where did you get this?"

"One of our regular freelance snappers took it. It may be worth a picture credit for her."

"You're not kidding!" He looked at the second picture, obscuring the body, but then went straight back to the first one.

"Does that solve your problem?" asked Spike, somewhat rhetorically. He wrote down the name Kat Bishop on the top sheet of the pages of copy, and made his way back down to reception to sign out, and then out to his car.

Driving back home, he weighed up what to do about going to the police. He knew it had to be done, but he wanted a clear head when he did it, and it had been a long day. A few hours sleep would put him in a better frame of mind, but when he finally had a chance to lie down and tried to leave his thoughts behind, he found himself staring at the ceiling.

Eventually he stopped trying to let go and used the opportunity to try to put events in some kind of order, to make sense of what he had seen, though there was no logic to any of it. He may have dozed off briefly, though not enough to forget the situation he found himself in and the prospect of what would come next.

As the first signs of daylight began to lift the gloom in his bedroom, he got up and washed and changed. It did seem as if he had only just come in, but there was an urgency about his movements now that made sleep seem like an indulgence. At least by leaving early he should avoid another confrontation with the taxi driver, with or without his wife.

At the police station he asked what time the chief inspector would come on duty, and was told that he had started already. In a way it didn't surprise him. In their few meetings he had exuded an air of one who rises early and operates at maximum efficiency, his desk so uncluttered that it could pass for a department store demonstration one adorned with only a few essential items, sufficient to suggest to potential buyers how it might look when installed. A phone call from the desk sergeant to his boss had the desired effect, and a button pressed under the counter sounded a buzzer that allowed Spike access through the staff security door.

The tiled floor of the stairs and the corridor that it led to, with its rooms on either side, was familiar to Spike, as was the face of the uniformed officer behind his desk who bid him "Enter!" when he knocked alongside the nameplate.

"You've saved my officers an errand to bring you here," said Chief Inspector James Parish, 'Jim' to his friends. "I think you know what I mean." Spike nodded. "Would you like to tell me why you were in a wood on the outskirts of Bartown late yesterday evening, Mr Pike?"

If the formal wording of his name was intended to make him aware of the seriousness of his situation, it succeeded. "I was following up a story."

"The missing person case?"

"Yes."

"What were you hoping to find?"

"Any clues as to what had happened to him."

"In the dark? In a place that my officers had just searched extensively?"

"They missed the shoe the first time around." Spike hoped that the remark wouldn't antagonise the officer, but it needed saying.

"And you just happened to come across a body, you and your photographer?"

"We got lucky."

"You had better hope that your luck lasts then, because the person who finds the body usually becomes the chief suspect. Did you see anyone else during your nocturnal visit to the scene of the crime?"

Spike thought about the figure with the suitcase and the man with no name. He could argue that he wasn't at the crime scene itself when he saw them, on his first visit to the lay-by earlier in the evening. Nor had he seen Harry Dixon until he'd looked at the photograph. "No, but I didn't hang around." He hoped that the chief inspector didn't know he'd been there twice.

Jim Parish looked at him intently, no doubt applying the skills he had learned for recognising when someone was lying. "That's a pity. It could have been to your advantage if you had seen someone else there, to shift the focus of blame."

The chief inspector got up and crossed the room to where there was a bookcase against one of the walls. He bent down to look at the row of spines on one shelf and after a few seconds found what he was looking for. He selected a book and opened it at the contents page, to look up the number of the chapter he wanted.

"Do you go fishing?" he asked.

Spike was a little surprised. "No, not since I was a child."

"Perhaps you should. It's a popular pastime. Helps you to relax." He turned the book over, so that the cover faced upwards. "*A Guide to the Freshwater Fishes of Britain*," he read. He turned to the chapter that he had marked with his forefinger. "'The Pike,'" he read, a sense of drama in his voice, like an actor intoning from the front of a stage. "'Sometimes known as the freshwater shark, nicknamed by anglers the crocodile among coarse fish species, the pike is a cold-hearted killer that lies in wait to ambush its prey and dispatches it in an instant, showing a swift and merciless disregard for its victim, which often include its own species.'" He looked up from the page and closed the book with snap. "Are you a cold-hearted killer with a merciless disregard for your victim, Mr Pike?"

"I didn't kill Geoffrey Fellows, if that's what you think." Even when facing questioning, Spike couldn't lose his reporter's instinct to probe. "I take it that it was him?"

"We won't know until a formal identification has taken place, but in the meantime, I would suggest to you that you let us know if you intend to travel outside the local area in the next few days, in case we need to bring you in for further questioning. And my advice to you would be to make preliminary arrangements to be represented legally, in case evidence comes to light that suggests involvement by you in what has taken place."

Spike sensed that he was free to go, if not off the hook entirely. He made his way out of the room to the sound of his footsteps, no pleasantries such as 'Goodbye' or 'Take care' being accorded to someone now branded a potential criminal.

It was still too early for the office staff to be in, but Spike found a note tucked behind the roller of his typewriter with his name written on the front. It was from Tom, telling him that the flowerpot man, Charles Appleby, had been in touch to say that he was being sued by his postman and would be fighting the case. Tom wanted Spike to go and see him to put together a story along the lines of 'postman delivers damages claim.'

It would be a welcome change to think about something other than the missing person case, so after a stop for breakfast, Spike took the road that the ambulance had used when he had been following it, and parked where the crew had loaded the injured man inside.

Charles Appleby was carrying a bag of rubbish out to his dustbin when Spike's car drew up in front of his house. He looked up and recognised the reporter, waiting for him to come down the drive and inviting him inside.

Mr Appleby spread documents from a folder on his dining room table to show to Spike, among them letters from his postman's solicitors outlining his case. He also had letters from a firm of solicitors that he had engaged to defend himself against the action, most of which contained columns of figures with pound signs in front of them.

"You wouldn't believe what they charge just for writing a letter or making a phone call," complained an exasperated Mr Appleby. "It's eye-watering what they want me to pay, and that's without having been found guilty. They are just lining their pockets at my expense, but I won't stand a chance in court if I'm not represented.

"Look at this one." He held up a letter on the headed notepaper of Carter, Brice and Elms listing all the different ways in which he could arrange to pay their charges, from forking out a hefty fee up front and seeing it whittled down until he had to stump up another big sum, or paying an hourly rate, including time spent acquainting themselves with the facts of the case. Below both was a disclaimer saying that all figures were estimates and they could not rule out the possibility that the true cost could be higher. "They haven't even got round to asking me what happened yet," moaned Mr Appleby. "Everything they've sent me so far has been about paying them."

For Spike it had a familiar ring. He recalled being similarly dismayed when he had dealt with solicitors during his divorce, but he shook his head appropriately when perusing the correspondence, for the benefit of his host.

"Can you afford it?" he asked, sympathetically.

"I'll have to. I haven't got much choice."

"If you win, you'll get your legal costs paid by the other side," said Spike, trying to sound optimistic.

"And if I lose, I'll have to pay theirs. The only winners will be the lawyers, because they get paid whatever the outcome."

"If I write a story about you facing a big bill because your postman fell over a flowerpot, I'll need to approach your solicitors for a comment."

"Whatever you think best. If you can persuade them to explain why they charge so much, that would be nice."

"There may be a way of doing that," Spike told him.

The firm of Carter, Brice and Elms had an office in the high street of Bartown, not far from the newspaper's premises. Spike climbed the dozen or so stone steps and pushed open the glass-centred connecting door, which had the company name painted on it in gold lettering.

A young woman looked up from her typing and smiled in welcome. "Can I help?"

"Would it be possible to see someone about being legally represented?"

"Yes, of course. Let's see. Mr Brice is available. I can ask if he's able to help." She took Spike's name and rang an extension number. Soon he was sitting in an upstairs room facing a large man seated behind an ornate desk, his bright red braces standing out against the sober stripe of his shirt as he leaned across to offer a fleshy hand for Spike to shake.

"How can we be of assistance?" he asked.

"I've been advised by the police that it might be in my best interests to seek legal advice while being questioned in relation to a crime that has been committed. I thought I would find out what would be involved and how much it might cost."

Mr Brice certainly seemed interested. "What is the nature of the crime?"

"A body has been found and it looks like murder."

The eyebrows on the other side of the desk began to be raised, before their owner remembered his professional detachment and lowered them quickly. "What is your connection with the crime?"

"I found the body. I was seen by someone there and they told the police before I could report it, making them suspicious."

"Did you know the deceased?"

"I'd never spoken to him, though I guessed from what I'd read in the papers that it was the missing local man that police were looking for."

"I wouldn't trust what you read in the papers. In my experience, what they can't find out they just make up anyway."

Spike wasn't about to let him get away with that. "Really? Some might say that they are a force for good, standing up for ordinary people and helping to fight injustice."

"If you'll forgive me for sounding cynical, I think the majority of them are happy to twist the facts to make a good story, but we are digressing. Are you able to explain your actions to the police regarding your discovery of the body?"

"Not entirely to their satisfaction, hence the advice of getting represented."

"In that case it might be best to have in place some legal cover. We can offer you our services on the basis of an hourly rate, which comes at a lower price but with no set boundary as to how many hours will be required, or we can charge you a set fee, which is at our higher rate, but this offers the reassurance that the amount that you pay will be fixed." He slid an A4 sheet of prices across the desk towards Spike, who intercepted it and read down the columns.

Spike winced, though he had seen the figures earlier. "Those charges seem rather high."

"I think you'll find that they are commensurate with what most competent partnerships in the county would charge. Although we are not the cheapest, we are by no means the most expensive, and we pride ourselves on providing a first-rate service."

"Do you ever get clients raising concerns about the cost?" asked Spike.

"The majority of our clients recognise that a high standard of service needs to be rewarded accordingly," he was told.

"But some don't?"

"In the rare cases when budget constraints dictate that prospective clients need to take their business elsewhere, we accept that sometimes alternative arrangements need to be made by them by looking further afield."

Spike had a counter argument. "But whereas some trades can justify their charges by citing rising costs of energy or raw materials, I dare say your fees are based more on what you can get away with."

Mr Brice was beginning to realise that the person sitting opposite him may have changed his mind about engaging the services of his firm.

"If you would like time to consider whether you want to be represented by us, by all means give the matter some careful thought before making a decision, and perhaps discuss the matter with your partner. However, I would suggest that from what you have told me, it would seem that you may be in need of someone to advise you legally sooner rather than later."

It was only when Spike was outside on the street that he switched off the tape recorder in his lapel pocket, giving the recording a brief playback to ensure that it had captured the quotes that he needed to write the flowerpot man story.

Chapter 12

Carl was installed behind his desk when Spike entered the reporters' room and hung his jacket on the back of his chair, though he didn't sit down until he had glanced inside the editor's office, and thankfully found it empty.

"Well, if it isn't Sherlock Pike, solver of great mysteries ahead of the police."

Spike had wondered whether Carl had heard, but he wondered no longer. "You've been speaking to someone at the *Evening Post*."

"I had to ring them about a story I was writing, but yours had already grabbed all the attention. Not to mention the picture. How come you were down there before the coppers arrived?"

"They asked me the same question. I told them that I was looking for clues in the missing person case. Jim Parish even suggested I might have killed someone to get the story."

"He's just looking to collar someone. Mind you, it's been a while since we've had a murder to write about around here. You could just imagine bumping someone off to get a story like that. You didn't see anyone around at the time behaving suspiciously?"

There it was again, the same question. Spike had to be careful when answering, but he hadn't seen anyone else 'at the time'. "No, but it was dark and we weren't there for long."

"What's your next move?"

"Go and see the widow and then wait for the autopsy, to see whether it is murder, and maybe visit the college again to get their reaction." One of the ladies from the front desk came in with the first editions of the *Evening Post*. "Oh, and have a look at how my story has turned out."

Both Spike and Carl laid their broadsheet copies of the paper out, propped up against the front of their typewriters and began reading the lead story.

The headline was: 'Town bypass gets go-ahead'. Spike turned inside to see the next spread of pages, but learned that: 'Pay talks stalled with fire station staff', and 'Cyclist sets out on epic charity ride'.

He turned another page, but more in hope than expectation, and found just more in a similar vein. He looked across to Carl to share his disappointment, and the fact that he was smiling back at him sent a chill through his body. Seeing Spike's face made Carl convulse with laughter, bending over forwards in his chair, which was sideways on to his desk, so that his head was almost level with the surface. "Your face..." he managed to get out between bouts of laughter. "... like a hungry cat that's been given an empty bowl."

"What?" Spike was clinging to the hope that things weren't as they seemed.

"You've been had. Hook, line and sinker. There wasn't a body. It was a fake."

As the realisation took hold, Spike wanted to ask who had done it, but he didn't need to pose the question. "I bet I can guess who it was who put it there."

"He got the chief inspector to play along with it. They're old friends, from their school days."

"And the bloke with the suitcase in the boot of his car?"

"He helps out with the local dramatic society. They had a body in their props store left over from a Tom Stoppard play they put on."

Spike no longer felt like writing his flowerpot man story. Instead, he put his jacket on and headed back outside, telling Carl as he left: "I want to see it for myself."

The wood looked a lot less sinister in daylight, especially now that he knew what it held, or didn't hold. There were no police forensic teams combing the crime scene, and no uniformed men keeping press and public at a distance.

The door to the hut opened with his key, and there inside was the 'body', hanging from a cord attached to the roof beam. Spike stepped inside, his footsteps sounding loud on the wooden floor as he crossed the room to take a closer look.

It was a good fake, realistic even at close quarters, made bulky and heavy by the cloth material stuffed inside, like a giant doll, but without any facial features. Spike gave it a prod to see how solid it was, and than stepped back and swung an angry kick at the legs, making it sway like a punch-bag. He wished it had been Harry Dixon hanging there for him to aim at, maybe even just hanging there; that would be enough. But more than that, more than seeing his tormentor suffer, he wanted revenge.

He closed the door behind him, listening to the latch click, not needing to hurry. As he walked back along the trampled path through the trees, he noticed something bright in the undergrowth. At first, he thought that it was a flower or a piece of litter, and he almost ignored it and walked on. But something made him glance a second time, and he realised that it wasn't the bright red of a flower but of a piece of material.

It was close to the path, in the undergrowth, and Spike walked the two or three paces to where it was almost hidden. He reached down and picked it up, curious as to what it was. As he turned it over in his hand, he could see that it was some kind of handle, with a bit of tartan cloth attached where it had torn free. It seemed unconnected with anything that he had seen before, but then his mind pictured the suitcase being dragged out of the car and how in the low light he had noticed that it had been red, perhaps even tartan.

Spike put the handle in his pocket, perhaps expecting to throw it away at some stage when it had proved irrelevant. Better to have it safe somewhere if he needed to see it again than to regret tossing it back into the vegetation because he'd thought it was nothing important.

He sat in his car at the lay-by for a while, trying to organise his thoughts. There was still a missing person to find. For all Harry Dixon's wind-ups, that hadn't changed, and he had as much chance of getting some clue as to what had been going on than his rival, perhaps more chance given that he had tracked down the man with no name. And then there was Sapphire. He looked at his watch. All of a sudden, he found himself in need of a drink.

The lounge bar at the Horse & Barge was only moderately busy when Spike stepped inside. Sapphire was giving a customer his change and laughing at something that he'd said. It was only when Spike's eyes had adjusted to the low light levels that he realised who it was. The man picking up one of the two pints of beer in front of him on the bar and taking a pull from one was Harry Dixon, and on his left, being passed the other pint, was Carl. They didn't move away from the bar but carried on chatting to Sapphire, and Spike recalled that he had mentioned her working part time in the pub in his piece in the paper.

Both men had their backs to him, so Spike was able to make his escape unseen, back out through the doorway that he had just come through. There was one place that he knew he could escape from them and that was in the office. By the look of them they wouldn't be back for a while.

He still had the flowerpot man story to write, and it was while he was doing that in the empty reporters' room that Tom came in. Thankfully he hadn't heard about the night's activities and he was more interested in how Spike had got on talking to the man with no name. As he told him, Tom fetched a press release from his desk with an address scribbled on it. It was from a publishing house in London explaining that a new book by a local children's author was about to be published, and to ring if the paper wanted to meet him.

Tom had rung them and been given an address for Colin Mears, the writer of the latest in a series of woodland animal adventure stories, along with permission to pay him a visit.

Spike handed over his flowerpot man story in exchange for the contact details provided by Tom, and then set off to find the man in question, with the words: "Maybe he knows something about our missing teacher," sounding in his ears.

Spike slowed his car to a pace that allowed him to read the house numbers on the gates or walls of the properties, those that had them, until he reached a particularly overgrown front garden. He drove past, not seeing any number, but put the car into reverse when he discovered that the number on the next one was two digits higher than the one that he wanted.

He had to stand on tip-toes to get between the hedge and the boundary fence to reach the front door, where the thick stem of a wisteria climber twisted up the wall and over the doorway. A smart woman with a bob of blonde hair answered the door, and Spike introduced himself, explaining his purpose.

"You'll find my husband around the back," she said, on the patio. "You won't see him at first, but if you think you're lost, you're on the right track."

Spike battled his way through more vegetation around the side of the house, to be met with a jungle at the rear. There were trees that had grown to full height in the distance, where birds flitted from bough to bough, and tall shrubs everywhere, their branches and big leaves crisscrossing as if trying to stop anyone from getting past. Spike parted them as gently as he could, not knowing where he was going and, just as the man's wife had said, he was beginning to think about turning back when he came to a clearing caused by the flagstones of a patio.

On it were four metal chairs and a matching round table. One of the chairs was occupied by a man with untamed hair and a bushy beard. On the table in front of him was an A4 notepad, in which he was writing with a ballpoint pen. Spike approached tentatively, not wanting to disturb his creative flow, but his footsteps on the stones betrayed his arrival and the man looked up, a vague expression on his face at first as he readjusted his thoughts.

Spike made his introductions again, offering his hand, and the man stood up to welcome him. "Call me Colin," he suggested, having been addressed as Mr Mears. "Mears isn't my real name, anyway. I like to keep my professional activities separate from my private life, so I adopted a pseudonym. At school my nickname was 'Ears', for obvious reasons." Now that he mentioned it, Spike noticed his rather prominent appendages. "So My Ears became Mears. Have a seat."

Spike drew up a chair as the man apologised for the unkempt state of his garden. "Normally when you ask visitors whether they found your home okay, you mean the journey to your address, but in my case, it applies more to the journey from my front door."

As he was speaking, his wife appeared, somehow managing to negotiate the rampant foliage with a tray containing three glasses and a jug of fruit juice alongside two bottles of beer and a dish of nuts.

"Ah, perfect timing," said Colin. "You've met my wife, Maureen."

Soon Spike was enjoying that rare privilege of being able to combine work with the pleasure of relaxing with a drink, made all the more welcome having recently experienced the disappointment of entering a pub and leaving a few seconds later just as thirsty as when he had gone in.

What made the hospitality of his host all the more acceptable was that alcohol always made interviewees more effusive in their answers, loosening their tongues and lowering their inhibitions. He had often mused how drinking and journalism had become so closely intertwined, and he was firmly of the belief that it was because one 'oiled the wheels' of the other in more ways than one.

The three chatted about the forthcoming book and how the animal characters had sprung from his love of nature. He claimed that the prolific condition of his garden was born out of this inclination, though his wife suggested that when he went outside it was either to write or to garden, and usually it was the writing that won.

At one stage a blue-tit alighted on the table, which was an all-weather iron one with an intricate pattern of shapes cut out of it, through which the patio was visible below. The bird landed near the edge of the table and then hopped its way to the dish of nuts, selecting one and then flying off in a blur of wings that made a noise like a paper fan being opened.

The couple were ready for Spike's look of surprise. "That's one we hand-reared," he explained. "We found it on the ground before it had fledged, having fallen from its nest, so we took it in and fed it until it was able to fly."

When Spike had enough material on his host's writing career, he mentioned the case of the missing teacher turned author, asking whether he had ever come across him.

"We were both once in the same writers' group, when we were learning the trade and bouncing ideas off other members, though we didn't keep in touch after we left."

"What was he like, as a person?" asked Spike.

He and his wife looked at each other. Eventually he said, in a jocular manner: "Perhaps its best not to speak ill of the dead."

Maureen corrected him immediately. "You don't know that's what's happened."

But her husband wasn't contrite. "Well, it looks that way. And it's not that surprising really."

"In what way?"

Colin Mears took another mouthful of beer. "He was always flying by the seat of his pants."

Maureen was ready to interpose again. "It was all hearsay. We never knew for sure."

But Colin continued. "His wife knew about it, the rumours of the other women, but she took him back if it was true."

"Other women?"

"Let's just say that the writer's hut in the woods wasn't just for pen and paper activities. It was a bit of a rendezvous for assignations."

"You don't know that definitely," said Maureen.

"Why else would you buy a wood and set up a pied-à-terre away from prying eyes and a safe distance from home? He always had a roving eye when we were out somewhere, so when he went missing, we thought it looks like his past has caught up with him."

"Did you know any of the women that he was interested in?"

"I don't think they would have lasted long with Geoffrey. I think he liked to 'trade them in for a new model with fewer miles on the clock'. But as I say, that was a while ago. He may have changed his ways as he got older and wiser." As he took another swig of beer he thought for a moment. "There was one person in the writers' group who took a shine to him. He used to give her a lift home."

"Do you remember her name?"

"Yes, but only the first name. I only remember that because it was the same as my wife's, Maureen."

Spike thanked the couple for their time and hospitality, and then fought his way back out to his car on the road outside, feeling as if he had returned to reality with the gardens around him now a more normal size. As he sat inside, he had an idea. He'd never liked the phrase 'to kill two birds with one stone,' but it came to mind as he glanced at his notebook, making sure that he had everything with him before driving away.

Chapter 13

The main library in Bartown was on the road south from the centre of town, with a small car park alongside the red brick building. The steps up to the entrance led to two separate doors inside about a dozen feet apart, one on the far left and the other on the far right, bearing the words 'Entry' and 'No entry' on their varnished wood, a one-way system being in place. Spike pushed the left hand of the two inner doors open and let it rock back and forth to its closed position again behind him.

A lady in a pink cardigan behind the counter came to help, and he asked if he could view the electoral register for the town, his voice automatically adopting that hushed tone reserved for libraries and places of worship. It must have been a routine request because she didn't enquire as to why he wanted to see them, but simply led the way to a shelf in the reference department and pointed to a line of ring binders with letters printed on their spines showing the sections of the alphabet that each one covered.

As he thanked her, Spike asked if she knew anything about the town's writers' group, thinking that she may have a contact number for someone involved. Moving past him to further down the shelf, she took down a box file and opened it, showing an extensive collection of their newsletters, the most recent one, from a few weeks ago, on top. When she said: "They publish them twice a year," Spike spirits were given a lift. Judging by the number of copies he'd seen in the file, there would be several years worth of outpourings.

He smiled at the lady and let his tone of surprise reflect his appreciation at her knowledge and helpfulness, feeling like adding as she left: 'I'll add you to my Christmas card list,' such was his mood of gratitude.

In the electoral register he found the road where the man with no name lived, and scanned the list until he came to the number of the flat that he occupied. The name alongside it was Jake Cousins. For some reason that seemed to fit, and Spike jotted it down next to the address he had in his notebook. None of the other names of the occupants of the flats meant anything to him, so he replaced the binder and turned his attention to the writers' group file.

He lifted out the full collection of newsletters, hoping that he would find the date of the earliest printed at the top of the page of the oldest one, but they bore no clue as to when they had been printed, just a number, indicating their order.

On the front page was a list of the 'homework' projects to be undertaken by the members in that period, and the names of books that would be read and discussed, along with the names of some guest speakers. It was when Spike turned over the page that he found some samples of their work, in particular poetry, and even a limerick competition winner, and then what he had been hoping for, the names of the current members.

Spike ran his finger down the list and stopped when he came to the name 'Maureen Farrell'. There was no mention of Geoffrey Fellows or Colin Mears, but when they moved on, she may have continued to attend. Perhaps it was wishful thinking, but Spike allowed himself to hope.

As he put the pages back in the file, he glanced at the most recent one, seeing the name of a Mrs Nesbit in the list of current members, which he jotted down.

He spied the latest copy of the Bartown telephone directory on a shelf nearby, and a flick through to the Fs showed several Farrells, none of them with a letter M. But by going back to the electoral roll and checking each of the addresses, he found an Alan Farrell living at the same address as a Maureen Farrell, at 39 Askew Avenue, and quickly wrote down the road name and number, along with the phone number from the directory.

It was with a sense of satisfaction that he replaced the reference material he had used on the shelves and gave the lady another smile and a thank you when she looked up from her filing as he passed her on his way out through the exit. As he stepped outside into the sunshine, he reflected not for the first time how even the smallest of successes can change one's mood and transform a day that looked like turning into a disaster into one on which good progress was made.

Having got the children's author story in the bag earlier, Spike felt he had earned the right to indulge himself with a speculative visit to Askew Avenue, and after a quick look at the Bartown street map he kept in the glove compartment of his car, he made his way there, stopping outside number 39.

There was no car in the drive, but when he rang the bell, he heard a noise inside that sounded like an internal door being opened, and soon the front door was answered by a small lady with a dark bob of hair and a small, almost girl-like frame. "Sorry to bother you," said Spike. "I'm looking for Maureen Farrell."

She looked a little surprised. "Yes, that's me."

"I'm doing some research into writers' groups and I had your address passed on to me as someone who was once an active member of the Bartown group."

"That was a while ago. I haven't been a member for a few years."

"I've spoken to someone from the modern era, a Mrs Nesbit, I just wanted an insight into how things were a few years ago."

She hesitated for a moment, uncertain, but decided that he looked like someone who could be trusted. "Oh. Okay. Would you like to come in?"

Sitting in an armchair opposite Mrs Farrell, his notebook resting on his knee, Spike jotted down details in shorthand as she replied to his questions. She told him how she first became involved and how long she had been a member, and what her experience had been of regular attendance.

"Did you have any members who went on to be published?" he asked.

"Yes, two of the group are now published authors," she said proudly. "You could tell from what they read to us that they were serious about improving and being successful."

"Who were they?"

"You probably haven't heard of them, because their books were only for a niche market, but they were successful to us. One was the children's author Colin..., Colin... My memory isn't what it was." She looked down at the carpet, trying to eliminate distractions as she pushed her brain to recall the surname. "Mears," she suddenly blurted out triumphantly. "Yes, that's it, or it was his pen name anyway, and the other was Geoffrey Fellows."

"Did they share with you any of their advice on how to achieve their goal?"

"It wasn't until after they'd left that they had books published. They came to learn and try out ideas on the rest of the group and then went away to put their ideas into practice."

"They didn't come back afterwards to tell you about it?"

"No," she said, rather wistfully. "That would have been nice, but we rather lost touch."

"They could have joined forces and organised a sort of reunion."

"I don't think they would ever have done that," said Maureen, quickly. "I think they'd have ended up killing each other. They didn't see eye to eye."

"They were rivals?"

"Not exactly, but they found it hard to agree with each other on anything. There was always a bit of tension in the air when one or other was reading. You could almost feel the disapproval of the other one. It seemed to me when they left that they'd had enough of one another, and that was as much a reason for leaving as having learnt as much from the group as they could. They were very different characters. Colin was very much someone who had sudden bouts of inspiration and was coming up with wild ideas, whereas Geoffrey was very matter of fact, not a creative sort of person at all, very much a teacher who stuck to the script. He would do meticulous research and then adhere closely to it in what he was writing. I found Colin's creativity more inspiring."

She suddenly became aware that she had been allowed to open her mind to a stranger, and she straitened herself, even physically, curbing her instinct to share more of her thoughts. "You may not know, but Geoffrey has gone missing. It's been in the local paper. Everyone's hoping that he is found safe and well."

Spike sensed that the moment of being allowed into her confidence had passed, and that her mind was focused on the here and now and not the past any longer. He had seen it many times during interviews, when the stream of golden quotes had been reduced to a trickle and then stopped altogether as the person opposite him became self-aware once more.

"What organisation did you say you were working for?" she asked, aware now that there was a gap in her knowledge of him.

"It's a research company that wants to know about people's leisure activities. It's part of a nationwide survey."

"Oh. Okay."

Spike put his notebook in his pocket and got up.

"Well, it's been nice meeting you," she told him.

"Me, too," he said. "I live locally, so maybe our paths will cross again. Thanks for your time."

As Spike drove away, he pondered the conflicting descriptions of Geoffrey Fellows that he had heard in the same afternoon. They couldn't both be right, which meant that one of the people who had provided them had been lying, but which one, and why? He looked at his watch. It should be safe to return to the office now and write the story on the children's author, before planning what to do next.

But on his way, he took a short detour past the lay-by alongside the wood where Geoffrey Fellows had his writing hut, to see whether there was any sign of activity, and as he drew level with the parking area he noticed something that made him pull over, the engine still running as he got out to look more closely. He picked it up and then out of his pocket he took another one exactly the same, a suitcase handle with a piece of torn tartan fabric attached.

Chapter 14

As Spike pulled up in the street outside the newspaper's offices, he spied a red sports car parked a little way down the road. He sat in his car for a few moments, considering going home to write the story. The portable typewriter in a case that he would bring out to knock out a news item in the evening to take into the office the following day seemed to be getting a lot more use lately.

But he knew that he was hiding from confrontation and would need to face the occupant of the desk in front of him at some stage. Better that he was prepared and had time to gather his thoughts than to be taken by surprise, lost in his work only for the door to open and the person he least wanted to see to be there in front of him.

He thought for a little while longer, running through the possible scenarios in his mind, and then got out of his car to climb the old stone steps once more.

In the reporters' room he found Harry Dixon seated at the desk in front of his, typing busily. He looked up as Spike came in, and a smile crept onto his face. To Spike, it seemed as if he was remembering the previous night's activities. Spike's plan, if you could call it that, was to say as little as possible, to avoid being drawn into an angry exchange of words.

"How's it going?" asked Harry, still smiling, as if he were still enjoying a very funny joke.

"As well as could be expected."

"Not still in shock, then?"

"I'll get over it."

"Or angry?"

"I think I've gone past anger. I'm on to whatever takes its place."

Harry warmed to the theme. "What are the emotional stages we're told we all feel when something dramatic comes our way: shock, realisation, fear, anger, puzzlement and revenge?"

"I'll let you know when I reach revenge." He sat at his desk, as if preparing to work, but he knew already that it wouldn't be possible here. "How did you know I'd be going to the hut?"

"I was with Jake when you rang him to arrange to call round. He told you he had someone coming round, but I was there already. I knew if he left just after you had been, that you'd follow him. He'll do anything for the price of a drink."

The casual way in which the name 'Jake' was thrown in, which had taken Spike so much digging to find, made him feel inadequate. He hadn't even been sure that Harry had sussed out the wrong number, but here he was on first-name terms.

"If it's any consolation, I've been impressed with how well you've been doing," Harry told him. "I've been in this game for a few years now and it can be hard work chasing a real story, especially with not much to go on, but you were making good progress."

Spike couldn't think of anyone he wanted compliments from less. Why did people for whom you had no respect think you wanted the benefit of their approbation? But it continued.

"You've got the makings of a good reporter. You just need to go that extra yard to make it all come together. It's easy when you're almost there to pull back and take stock and end up just short of where you want to be. The thing to remember is that in almost every profession – police, teachers, solicitors – there are rules about what you can and can't do, but not for journalists. We live by our wits and we can do what we like, if we've got the nerve. It puts us one step ahead of everyone else.

"Of course, there will always be people who will try to stop you. But you have to expect that. I always say that a news story is what someone doesn't want you to print; everything else is free advertising. The thing to do is to learn not to care what anyone else thinks, and not to think of the consequences of what you're doing. Just get a bit of steel in your backbone and I think you could make the grade."

If Spike had been stuck on 'puzzlement' in the spectrum of emotions, he had just moved up a notch. There was a calmness about him now that there hadn't been before. Something in him had changed. He had been holding on to an awareness of a need to behave responsibly and to curb his desire for revenge, but he had just let go, and it made him feel free.

He put his notebook back in his pocket and stood up, pushing his chair back under the desk. "I'm going to head off. Maybe you can buy me a pint some time, to wipe the slate clean."

"Sure thing," said Harry. "Maybe have lunch up at the Horse & Barge. The food's tasty up there, and so are the barmaids."

Spike gave a shudder as he walked back to his car. He had a story to write, in the comparative quiet of his room, and some thinking to do, but the pieces were beginning to fall into place now. It was always strange how they did that at the right moment, when the next step was needed, coming together just in time, as if whatever he was about to do was meant to be.

The following morning as he left home, even before Spike had reached his car, he knew something was wrong. It didn't look right as he walked up the drive towards it, and when he was in full view of it, he could see why. So much had happened in the past day and a half that he had forgotten about Jack Sprat the taxi driver, but the memory came rushing back now as he looked at his vehicle.

The whole car was lower than it should have been, and when Spike looked down at the tyres he could see that all four were flat, the rims of the wheels resting on the road. For a moment he thought perhaps they had been let down, and a bit of work with a pump would have got him back on the road, but when he ran his hand along the walls, he could feel the jagged 'wounds' of deep slashes to each one. From looking at the one-inch insertion points, he guessed that a sharp knife with a point to the blade had been used, one stab on each tyre being enough to render his car immobile.

He looked around him, but he knew that it would have been done a long time ago and the person responsible would be well away by now. It looked as if he would be walking in to work, stopping at the garage on the way. The alternative, of course, would be to take a taxi, but somehow that idea didn't hold any appeal.

It felt unusual for Spike to be walking into town early in the morning on a weekday, and his brain and body kept reminding him that something was wrong. Thankfully, it was dry, though still a little chilly. What little sunshine there was hadn't mustered sufficient strength to warm the cool morning air, though the exercise soon got his circulation going and he had achieved a gentle glow from the exertion by the time he reached the garage.

The same man that Spike had spoken to before was in the office at the far end of the workshop at the garage. Spike explained to him what had happened, and how he needed to have his car collected on a low-loader and brought in because it wasn't driveable. The man winced. "All four been done?"

"Unfortunately."

"Who d'you think? Kids?"

"No, a neighbour. He doesn't like me parking outside where I live. Says it's just for locals."

"He doesn't drive a taxi, does he?" the man asked. Spike nodded. "I bet I know who that is. Reckons if you weren't born here, you didn't ought to live here. Even if you were, but your parents weren't, that's enough for him to fall out with you. I can have a word for you, if you like."

Spike was impressed. "Really?"

"I know someone who can fix these things."

"How would he go about doing that?"

"A word from the right person will make him back off, someone he'll listen to. There are people who have influence. Leave it with me, and I'll get your car sorted so you can come and pick it up this afternoon." Spike handed him the keys and walked along the road to the office, all the time wondering whether Mr Fixit really did have another string to his bow.

When Spike told Carl about what had happened with his car, back in the office, it didn't seem to surprise him. He had been typing a story, but he broke off to give Spike the benefit of what he'd learnt on the subject. When he was sober, mostly in the mornings, his views were always worth hearing, so Spike gave him his full attention for once.

"I think they call it the 'chocolate box' configuration. Every town has one. It looks as if you've just caught a glimpse of it here. You can look around the town and think that what you see is what you get, but there's another layer underneath, and there aren't any soft centres on that hidden tray, they're all hard-boiled and likely to break your teeth.

"On any day, you see people going about their business, going to work, visiting the shops and the Post Office, but underneath there's a lot more going on than just collecting their groceries or buying some stamps. People are interacting on a whole different level, but it's all hidden from view.

"When we first came here, my wife wanted a set of garden furniture for the front lawn, so that we could sit outside when the weather was fine. We spent a while picking out something nice, which cost us a few bob, and a couple of days later I pulled back the curtains in the morning to find it all gone.

"I went to the police and they gave me a crime number, but nothing came of it until Sandra was talking to an elderly lady whom she'd been helping fetch her shopping while she recovered from a hip operation. Sandra mentioned what had happened, and the next day the whole set was back where it had come from on our lawn."

Spike looked dismayed. "But that's really sad if the only way to get left in peace in this place is if you know someone who's able to have a word and call off the heavy mob."

But Carl could see the logic. "In a perverse sort of way, it makes sense. If you've had something taken from you, why go to an unconnected body of people like the police for help when you can go directly to the section of society that has caused the problem in the first place to find a solution? If you've got a leaky bathroom tap, you don't go to your local restaurant and ask the pastry chef if he can help you with it, you call someone who's in that line of business."

"Why don't we write stories about it if it affects so many people's lives?" asked Spike.

"When you see the bill for your tyres you'll realise why. You wouldn't want one of those every week. It's bad enough being on the bottom rung of society, as journalists, in the public's eyes at least, alongside traffic wardens and debt collectors, without becoming a sitting target for the underworld as well. Best not to poke the hornets' nest."

Carl returned to the story he had been typing. "It's how society works. It's not what you know, it's who you know, and who you upset or don't upset. Maybe it always has been. As Esther Rantzen is fond of saying: 'That's Life!'"

Spike wandered through to where Tom was typing in his office and, as he handed over the pages of his story on the children's author, his boss had another excursion lined up for him. "There's a local conjurer who has just been accepted into the Magic Circle. He's got a show at the Winter Gardens at the moment. Can you go and see him and get a few details? Find out how he got started and where he hopes his career will go from here, that sort of thing."

Tom handed Spike a piece of paper with the details written on it. "He's expecting a visit some time this morning. Oh, and by the way," Tom added as Spike turned to walk away, "if you shake hands with him, make sure to count your fingers before you come away, in case there are any missing."

Spike smiled weakly. "I know someone like that, and he isn't a magician."

The Winter Gardens was walking distance from the office, on the edge of the town's main park, set back from the road down a set of steps that stretched for the full width of the building. There was a closed ticket office on the way in, with a glass window and a gap of a couple of inches at the bottom for tickets to be pushed through to customers, and an area that formed the foyer, with wooden benches, vending machines and litter bins. It had a certain functional glamour to it, having attracted a few famous-name acts over the years on their circuits around the country, but without the élan of the West End, the red brick of the walls having a provincial air about them, lest anyone making it there should get ideas above their station.

Spike wandered through to the auditorium, which reminded him of school plays, the rows of seating being all on one level about five feet below the stage, which had a set of steps at each end, to allow for any audience participation incorporated in the act.

On the stage there was a small group of people discussing something that involved them turning now and then to move their arms in descriptive, sweeping gestures to demonstrate something that was planned. As the group began to break up, Spike made his way forward to the front of the stage and addressed a tall man in jeans and a smart jacket who had remained there.

"I'm looking for Captain Marvo," he said, aware even as the words came out how absurd they sounded.

"You've found him," the man informed him.

Spike introduced himself and was invited up the steps to join his subject. As he passed the side of the stage, he spied a cage of doves and a small hutch containing a white rabbit. Marvo fetched a couple of folding chairs from the back of the stage and arranged them alongside the table.

Marvo, whose real name turned out to be Brian, told Spike about his childhood present of a magic set that made him want to learn the tricks, initially to entertain his family and friends but later to try to break into the profession as an escape from his dull job as a bank clerk. He was currently working part time, and his acceptance as a member of the Magic Circle was a major step towards his ambition of earning a living from magic full time.

It wasn't long before he was dipping in his pocket and producing a coin, which he could close in his fist, turn his hand over and then open again showing that it was empty. Like most entertainers, seeing his audience looking impressed made him want to do more tricks, and soon he was working his way through various examples of sleight of hand, from rolling the same coin over his knuckles and then underneath, to fanning a pack of cards with a flick of his wrist and shuffling them by splitting the pack in two and putting them back into one deck in a moment by bending them so that they meshed together with a satisfying flickering sound.

80

One trick particularly intrigued Spike, involving a ping-pong ball that he made disappear in his hand. Spike wondered how such a large object could be hidden right in front of him. Marvo offered to show him, so long as he didn't tell his readers how it was done. After making the ball disappear, he showed him the inside of the sleeve of his jacket, which had a small pocket sewn into the lining where the ball was visible, like an egg in a bird's nest. "It's just a matter of practice," he told Spike. "If you do something often enough, it becomes second nature and you can do it quickly enough so that no one can see it happening."

As they talked, Spike wondered whether the magician had ever analysed his need to entertain. Had he worked out why he wanted to be noticed and to earn people's interest and approval?

Marvo told him: "I think we all want to be liked. When we tell a joke or do someone a favour, we do it to see their reaction. We want to know that we have that power in us to produce the reaction we are looking for. I think what I do is just an extension of that. We are social animals that want to know that we can be liked. Some of us need it just a bit more often than others."

On the way back to the office, Spike pondered what he had said, not so much about wanting to be liked, but how if you practised something often enough you could get so good at it that no one could see you doing it. All he needed now was a small pocket sewn into the lining of one of his jackets. If only he knew someone who was a wizard at sewing.

When Spike reached the office to write the magician story, a message had been left that his car was ready to be collected, and Tom had another job lined up for him for when he'd fetched it. A local amateur gardener had won a national award for his prize blooms, so Spike was being asked to go along to meet him, and to take Kat with him.

He was braced for a big bill when he collected the car, but glad to be mobile once again, and grateful for the offer to do something to prevent a recurrence. Having to shell out for a set of new tyres was bad enough when they were probably due for a change soon anyway, but doing the same to replace a set of brand-new ones because it had happened again would be too much to bear.

As the garage owner put his Access card on the credit card machine and pulled the slider over it to make an imprint of the number, getting Spike to sign the slip and giving him the carbon copy, he repeated his earlier promise. "Leave it with me," he told him.

Spike picked Kat up at her home and together they made their way to an allotment on the edge of some open land opposite a long row of houses. On the way he broke the news to her about the hoax with the fake body, and who had been responsible.

"I hope you've got a suitable punishment in mind."

"Don't worry," Spike told her. "I'm working on it."

The prizewinning gardener was busy watering his flowerbeds. A fellow allotment holder, also a pensioner with shirt sleeves rolled up and loose-fitting trousers, which seemed to be the regulation uniform, pointed him out across the plots, and Spike hailed him as they approached.

Albert put down his watering can to shake hands with them both, wiping his fingers on a towel tied round his belt before administering his powerful grip. He showed them around his area of ground, pointing out each of the plants in turn, sometimes using latin names but more usually their common ones.

Kat got him to pose with the tall, spiky plants for which he had been given a notable merit, their deep blue colour standing out against the green of their circular, fan-like leaves. Bees thronged around them, crawling inside the pod-like flowers to reach the nectar before emerging and buzzing around to another. The loud noise made by their wings sounded to Spike as if they were making the sound 'Mmmmm!', like a child licking an ice-cream on a sunny day.

"I've always had a soft spot for lupins," Albert told them. "They seem to grow well in this soil, and I've managed to cultivate a large number of different colour varieties.

"It's handy growing them on this allotment, away from the houses and gardens, because people don't realise that they are poisonous – the leaves, the seeds and the seed pods. If you grow them in a garden, you can get your neighbour's cat chewing them, which could lead to problems. I wouldn't want a death on my hands."

Spike asked him how he developed new colours, and Albert took them along to his shed, where he kept his equipment. Around the walls were various rakes, spades and hoes, hanging from hooks attached to the wood, and on one of the benches was a large plastic storage box filled with old white envelopes, all stacked upright so that their contents didn't spill.

Albert took one out and on the front of the envelope was the name of the seeds inside, along with the date when they were harvested. "The great thing about lupin seeds is they keep almost indefinitely. Lots of seeds become inactive if they aren't planted within a couple of years, so you may as well throw them away, but the waxy coating on lupins keep them fresh for years."

He shook some out onto the rough skin of his palm and held them for the pair to see. Kat photographed him holding his hand out to the camera, with his face and filing system visible behind it, the shiny, dark seeds on display like mini magic beans in a pantomime performance.

As they were about to leave, Albert asked if either of them was a gardener, but they both said they didn't have the time or the space. He took an old empty envelope off a shelf and dropped a few seeds in it, folding it a couple of times to seal them in. "Here you go," he said. "Soak these in water overnight and put them in a small pot on a warm windowsill and see how you get on. You might be surprised at how much pleasure you get from them."

Spike dropped Kat back at her mother's front door. As she fetched her camera bag from the back seat, he dipped his hand in his pocket and pulled out the folded envelope. "Do you want some of these?" he asked her, rattling the envelope.

"I'm not bothered," she replied. "You'll probably have more use for them than I will."

Chapter 15

On his way back to the office, Spike stopped at the Horse & Barge. He was pleased to see that neither of his colleagues was present, and that Sapphire wasn't busy with customers.

"Just a flying visit," he told her. "Are you around at home this evening? This week's paper is being printed today and there are a couple of letters following up what I wrote about you last week, if you'd like to read them." She had a way of seeming to enjoy being given attention, though he suspected that it was part of her natural charm, which endeared her to customers as well as friends and casual acquaintances. He hadn't yet seen how she registered disapproval.

As she agreed to his visit, a group of customers approached the bar and he stepped aside, telling her he'd see her later. He had one more call to make before he got down to writing his stories from the morning over a sandwich from the shop close to the office.

But before he left, he approached the self-service display provided for diners to take cutlery, serviettes and cruets for their meal. A man was selecting what he needed to go with his food, and as he moved away, Spike picked up a small pepper pot and palmed it, in the manner of Captain Marvo, leaving without being noticed.

The Bartown College office was just inside the wide entrance, on the left just ahead of two steep flights of stone steps that led to the Great Hall above. Spike knocked on the door of the office and a woman's voice inside instructed him to come in.

The high-ceilinged room was bathed in sunshine from the large windows, with their pattern of small panes of glass held in place by lead muntins, offering a view of the grounds. The owner of the voice was seated behind a large desk festooned with paperwork. She looked up, pen in hand, as he entered.

Spike had met her once before, when interviewing the headmaster about Geoffrey Fellows, and the look she gave him, with its flicker of partial recognition, suggested that he wouldn't have his identity challenged.

As he reintroduced himself, the partial recognition transformed into the full version, and he was able to progress to his request. "Would it be possible to tell me whether someone was ever a pupil at the college?" he asked. "I'm putting together a story on Old Bartownians and I wanted to see whether he qualified as one."

Spike hoped she wouldn't ask him why he hadn't put the question to the man himself, as the headmaster might have done, but she was trained in acceding to requests rather than challenging them. After thinking for a moment, having started to rise from her chair and then paused as her brain switched from physical to mental activity, she completed the manoeuvre and walked to one of the wooden filing cabinets against the far wall.

"What's his name?" she asked.

"Jake Cousins," Spike told her.

She took out a folder marked with the letter 'C' and began perusing a list of names, alongside which were the start and finish dates of all of the attendees.

"We had a Jacob Cousins. Could that be him?"

"When did he leave?"

"Five years ago."

"No address or picture?" Spike knew he was pushing his luck.

"I'm afraid not." She closed the file, indicating that she had done her best with the resources at her disposal.

"Not to worry," said Spike, trying not to sound disappointed. As he was about to thank her and leave, he glanced up at the wall and noticed a row of school photographs. Lines of pupils in smart uniforms, the front ones seated and the rows behind standing on a terrace, stared dutifully at the camera, and below them, on the base of the photo, was the school year date.

"Is there one of those for the year that Jacob Cousins was last here?" asked Spike.

The secretary was seated again, but she rose and went to a different filing cabinet. After a few moments of searching, she pulled out an image, with its protective flap of cover paper, bearing the right year.

"Might I have a photocopy of it?" asked Spike. Once again it seemed that it was her role to serve and not to question. The copier hummed into motion, and after the bright light seeping from under the edge of the lid had traveled the length of the machine and back again, Spike had a black-and-white reproduction in his hands. He was profuse in his thanks as she replaced the photo in its home in the cabinet. He wouldn't be leaving empty handed after all.

Carl was in the reporters' room when he reached the office, and judging by the fumes from the cup of coffee that he was sipping, it had been flavoured with more than milk and sugar. When he had been imbibing, which was more often than not, he was even more given to sprinkling his conversation with quotations.

"All right? How's it going?" he asked.

Spike put his head around the door to Tom's office, but it was empty. "Tom not around?" asked Spike in reply. "Do you know where he is?"

"Am I my brother's keeper?" quoted Carl. It was a reply that Spike had received before from him, and which still held a certain level of amusement, for although Carl was not a churchgoer, he was fond of making that particular jocular reference to Cain and Abel when the opportunity arose.

"What have you been up to?" he asked, after a swig of his 'coffee'. The sting of being taken in by the fake body was still raw for Spike, and so was the sight of Carl in the Horse & Barge with Harry Dixon. He didn't feel like sharing in a jokey exchange.

"Just a couple of stories that Tom gave me to follow up. That's why I wondered whether he was around."

"I think he may be at the printers, doing the final checks before the presses roll." Carl leaned back in his chair and positioned his feet on the corner of his desk, one on top of the other. "Such is the mantel of responsibility that accompanies authority and status, compensated for by a fat wad of a pay packet, while you and I enjoy a more unburdened existence, especially when he's away, but one that renders us of more slender means. As Wordsworth put it: 'The heavy and the weary weight of all this unintelligible world is lightened.'"

He took another pull on his coffee. "You must aspire to greater things than this one day, to get paid to tell other people what to do rather than spend your time getting ordered around like we do now?"

It was clear to Spike that his colleague was in a mood to chat rather than work, in the absence of an authority figure within earshot, and experience had taught him that on such occasions he would get little work done. "I can't see there being a vacancy any time soon," he told Carl, slipping his notebook back into his pocket, thinking to himself that what he really aspired to was some peace and quiet.

"'Be alert, for you do not know when that time will come,'" quoted Carl dramatically. "'It cometh as a thief in the night.'"

"I'm going to grab something to eat. I'll see you a bit later," Spike told him, the words: "'Godspeed ye hence, and return ye safely to these shores anon,'" sounding in his ears. He allowed himself a wry smile as he walked the short distance to the sandwich shop, though he hadn't allowed Carl to see it, lest it encouraged him. When you were in the mood, he could be very entertaining when he was lubricated to the point of being expansive with his views and theatrical in his delivery, but when you were the only sober one at the party, it was better to be elsewhere. Any slight meanness he might have felt at deserting him when he clearly craved an audience was negated by the knowledge that Carl would probably already be entertaining the ladies in the front office with his conversation, especially if the number of customers had dwindled to a trickle.

The baker's shop was just a few doors along the high street from the newspaper's offices, and it was somewhere that was always a pleasure to visit. Enticing odours of hot sausage rolls and pasties wafted out of the door, pulling customers in from the pavement as they were walking past. In winter, the warmth from the ovens alone was enough to bring people in out of the cold and inevitably to spend some money, and in milder weather it was the warmth of the welcome that attracted passers-by.

The shop was run by a lady known to everyone as Diane, but to Spike she had another name, due to her soft white face, which resembled a large dollop of dough. She reminded him of an advert on the television for Pillsbury products, in which an animated figure made from dough and shaped like a boy in a chef's hat promoted the firm's bakery items. He always thought of Diane as Mrs Pillsbury, and had to steel himself to avoid accidentally calling her that when he visited.

She had two daughters, Edwina and Edina, who formed a trio with her to charm customers already salivating at the sight and smell of the golden crusted baked offerings appearing from the ovens behind them.

———

Through the swing door there was a Mr Pillsbury, toiling over creating and baking their products, which the ladies displayed on the glass-fronted shelves beneath the counter. If you timed it right, your choice of purchase could be just emerging from the oven as you asked for it, and many a time when Spike had visited, he had passed a customer on their way out, breaking open the pastry of their paper-wrapped offering, steam rising from the ingredients enveloped within, a look of bliss transforming their features as they took a bite of the oven-fresh filling.

Spike placed his order, and with his food in one of the shop's blue-and-white striped bags he headed home, where the thought of uninterrupted time with his portable typewriter and his notebook felt irresistibly attractive, allowing him to withdraw into a cocoon of tranquility. The sound of the keys of his machine clattering would be like the marching feet of progress, and the thought that he had a visit to make later would provide an incentive to make good use of his time.

Back at home, when both stories were written, Spike glanced at the clock. He still had time to spare, so he reached into the pocket of his jacket and took out the pepper pot he had palmed at the Horse & Barge. He put a piece of sticky tape over the holes in the top and practiced holding it in his palm without any part of it being visible.

He fetched the envelope containing the lupin seeds and tipped a few out onto a sheet of paper. They looked like small beans, dark brown with a small white mark where they had been attached to the parent plant. He found a piece of sandpaper in a drawer of oddments and carefully filed the surface of one of the seeds, creating a fine dust on the paper. When he had rubbed most of the seed to dust, he did the same with the others, pinching them gently between the tips of his fingers to scrape them back and forth on the abrasive surface.

Then he took the lid off the pepper pot and held the paper by its edges so that the powder slid into a line on the sheet. He put the edge of the paper on the lip of the pepper pot and tapped the paper gently, sending the dust tumbling gradually into the pot.

After replacing the lid and tipping the unused stubs of seed in the bin, he put the pot in his pocket and washed his hands.

As he waited for what would be closing time in the office and the hum of traffic to rise as people on the road outside made their way home from work, he opened the copy of the school photo that he had been given at the college. He scanned the rows of pupils' faces, looking for a familiar one, and while there were two or three possible matches, none was obviously the face that he was seeking.

He tried to imagine the man with no name, now identified as Jake, in his younger days. It seemed easy to see the likeness when you were shown two pictures of the same person taken many years apart, but when you were presented with a puzzle to guess the face, none of them seemed to match completely.

The office should be empty now, and the delivery of this week's paper imminent. Before he left, Spike went into the kitchen and opened a cupboard, where he knew he would find a small salt and pepper cruet of his own. He took the pepper pot and put it into the pocket of a different jacket, one that he would be wearing tonight. With his key to the office on his house keychain, he had everything he needed.

In the office, Spike cut the string holding together the bundle of newly printed copies of the paper and took two off the top, folding them in half to make them easier to carry. He listened for a moment for any sounds coming from the reporters' room, behind the front office, but there was no clacking of typewriter keys or speaking on a phone. Just as well, thought Spike. He didn't want to get sidetracked.

On the way to Sapphire's flat, he planned what he would say, handing her the paper and working his way towards asking her a favour involving stitching a small flap in the lining of his jacket. But when he reached the door, there was a woman standing in front of the entrance, pressing one of the buttons for the flats inside. She went in as he bumped his car's new tyres up the steep kerb onto the parking area in front of the building, and he hoped that she had been summoning someone from one of the other flats. But even as he pressed the button and played back in his mind the image he had in his head of the position of the woman's arm when she had been ringing one of the bells, he had a feeling that his arm was at the same angle to the upright as hers had been.

There was no answer to his pressing of the button, and instead of trying a second time Spike took a few steps back and looked up at the window on the second floor. He thought he could see a light on in a room further back in the flat from the one nearest the front, but he couldn't be certain. When he knew that no one was going to respond, he folded the copy of the paper that he had brought and took out a pen, writing above the masthead: 'Sorry I missed you, Spike', before pushing it through the letterbox marked with the number of her flat, and making his way back to his car.

As he parked in the road outside the house where he lived, it felt as if it would take a miracle for his newly mended car to remain untouched overnight and still be in the same drivable state the following morning as when he left it, but it was. Perhaps Carl was right, and the underworld had made it known that he should be left in peace.

Chapter 16

The day when the week's newspaper appeared on sale was what Spike liked to call the 'Day of Reckoning', or 'Crash Helmet Day', since it was when most of the town read the paper and made known any grievances that they felt at the way in which their part in any of the stories featured had been portrayed.

People whose names had been misspelled or the wrong names applied to captions would pick up the phone or even march up to the offices brandishing their well-leafed copy of the paper, which they had shown to anyone who would listen to them, expressing their dismay and contempt.

Sometimes it was stories that you'd expected them to like that they took umbrage at, perhaps because an otherwise flattering report had got their age one year out and they were hurt that the whole town would think that they were a year older than was the case.

At other times the flak was expected and maybe even anticipated with a strategy of carefully chosen replies. Spike knew that when the solicitors that he had quoted concerning his story on the flowerpot man saw what he had written, they would be in touch to complain. In many ways it was the reactions that were expected that hurt the least, since he could be braced for the blow when it came, having developed a thicker skin in anticipation.

Tom came through from his office to the reporters' room with a note that he had made while on the phone. "I've just had a call from Carter, Brice and Elms saying they are unhappy about the story we've printed on the postman. Their Mr Brice says he wasn't aware that he was being interviewed by a reporter for an item in a newspaper. The phrase 'underhand tactics' got mentioned a couple of times."

It was at that moment that the door to the reporters' room opened and Carl and Harry Dixon walked in. "Morning all," said Carl. "I've had the VIP treatment today. Harry saw me walking in and gave me a lift in his sports car."

"Just don't expect me to be passing every day," was Harry's comment.

Tom continued where he had left off on the postman story fallout. "Did you tell him you were a reporter?"

"I would never have got inside the door if I had. I knew I needed a quote to balance what Charles Appleby had said about their charges, so going undercover was the best way of getting it. Is he saying that what I wrote wasn't what he said, or is he just miffed that the public have found out what he thinks?"

"What he is saying is that his firm advertise with us from time to time and that in future they may decided to take their business elsewhere."

Carl couldn't resist chipping in. "We can't let firms dictate to us what we can and can't print. The next thing they'll be telling us to run every story past them so that they can decide what they'll allow us to use."

Tom knew the counter argument to that. "But if the paper has no advertisers, it can't afford to pay our wages. The cover price alone is never enough."

Harry joined the discussion. "Advertisers need us as much as we need them. How else are they going to reach an audience? They may issue threats about canceling their ads, but when they want to drum up some business, they'll soon come crawling back."

"What did you tell him?" asked Spike, thinking that already maybe it was going to be one of those days.

"I suggested we could arrange some ad-feature coverage for them if a few local companies that deal with them advertise. It might smooth things over. He said he'd get back to me."

"I don't think he'll want me to be the one to write it," said Spike.

"He did mention something about a body and a possible murder case, which I didn't follow," said Tom. For once there was no one in the room keen to offer an opinion. "He seemed to think you'd made up a murder story to get to see him, but I told him you wouldn't stoop to that. I know you sometimes need to bend the rules to get your foot in the door, but I'd suggest that when you are dealing with solicitors it's best to play it straight or it could get very messy." He looked up at the others. "I don't know what you all think?"

Carl was the first to offer a suggestion. "I think readers expect us to use whatever legal means we can to get to the truth. That's what they pay the cover price to find out. It's no good faffing about debating the ethics of how you go about things when you need to know what's been going on."

Harry was of the same mind. "The end always justifies the means, in my book. People talk about what's in the paper to their friends, saying: 'You'll never guess what's happened.' What you won't hear them say is: 'You'll never guess the lengths one of the reporters went to, just to find out what had happened.'"

Carl couldn't resist a comic finale. "Just steer clear of words like 'bloodsuckers', 'parasites', 'vultures' and 'hyenas' when you're writing the ad-feature on Carter, Brice and Thingamy. That'd be my advice."

Spike gave Tom the stories he had written at home, and in return he handed him the customary piece of paper with details of a story that he wanted covered. On it he had written 'George Davison – beekeeper' along with his address and phone number.

"Can you go along and see this chap? He's chairman of the local beekeepers' association and he's just launched a range of products using produce from his hives and those of other members. Get a bit of background on his history and how he looks after his bees. It might make a story that's a bit unusual. He's around this morning if you've got nothing else arranged."

"That's not George Davison, is it?" Harry interjected. Both Tom and Spike looked at him but said nothing, which was taken by Harry to be an affirmation. "I've met George before, when he was giving a talk on my old patch. Nice chap. Give him my regards. If it makes a good yarn, maybe you can let us have a few lines for the *Evening Post*." Tom made his way back into his office as Harry continued. "Are we meeting for lunch?" He seemed keen to follow through with his suggestion of a rendezvous at the Horse & Barge. Carl looked up on hearing the mention of something that would involve what he sometimes referred to as 'a libation'.

Spike had temporarily forgotten about the arrangement and, more importantly, what it entailed. He felt his heart sink a little at the suggestion as the realisation returned, but Carl was already responding enthusiastically. As Spike agreed to a time, he told himself that he could back out of what he had planned at any stage. Just being there didn't necessarily mean it had to happen.

Spike found George Davison's cottage down a long lane so narrow he was hoping nothing would come the other way because it would be impossible to pass. The man in question was trimming his hedge, and he put down his shears when Spike's car pulled up alongside the drive.

George's thinning hair and grey sideburns suggested he was in his sixties, and though he wasn't slim, his frame indicated a body that was well used to manual work and easily strong enough for the more taxing jobs that his hobby, and now his business, required.

There was definitely something bee-like about him, the roundness of his body and hairiness of his chest and arms. It was something that Spike had noticed before, how people often matched the work that they did, just as pet owners often resembled their pets. Butchers were often red faced, and policemen so straight-backed and upright that they seemed to have a broom handle down the back of their trousers. You could almost guess what someone did for a living or match the person to their pet without any need to ask them.

Spike introduced himself and was greeted with a powerful grip from a surprisingly soft hand, which its owner later explained to him was the result of handling bees wax and honey every day. George showed him around his garden, pointing out the hives in the distance, and then took him on a walk around the margins of the farmland that surrounded his cottage.

"I don't own the fields, just the cottage," he told Spike. "But the farmer lets me use his fields for my hives and we both benefit from the arrangement."

In the low-ceilinged kitchen, George's wife, Marie, a similarly smallish and rounded woman, was busying herself pouring honey skillfully from a large saucepan into 1 lb jars bearing labels with his name and that of the local association. Elsewhere in the kitchen were containers of various brightly coloured substances ready to be dispensed into individual packs.

They left Marie to her pouring and walked through to his living room, where a pair of worn-but-comfortable armchairs faced a fire and Spike was able to take down some details.

Beekeeping for George had been a lifelong activity that had made him many friends but also taught him much about the natural world. He was clearly enthralled at the workmanship of bees and how they made their food, and indeed their own medicine, and co-existed with each other in close proximity, thriving by each knowing their role in the production process, including caring for the next generation of bees. He was also firmly of the view that when someone died, the bees had to be told or they would leave their hive.

He showed Spike some propolis, which was one of the products that he was selling, for customers to sprinkle on their breakfast cereal. Marie brought through some small dishes of honey with a plate of chunks of home-made bread for Spike to dip into the dishes and discern the difference between hives placed in fields of differing crops, each with its own floral undertones. Even the smell of the honey was distinctive, very different from the sweet but faintly chemical taste of mass-produced blended honey, which George said didn't deserve the same name.

As Spike finished the last of the chunks of bread, Marie reappeared with a tray of three small glasses and an opened bottle of clear liquid. She poured three measures of the sweet drink as George asked Spike if he had ever tasted mead. Spike admitted that it was a first for him, and the three toasted the bees, clinking their glasses, before Marie returned to her work.

With all the details he needed now in his notebook, Spike found himself nestling down in the armchair, no longer needing to keep directly upright to be able to write with his notebook balanced on his knee.

As they talked and sipped, the time passed quickly, and it was only when Spike was offered a second refill that he became aware of how he ought to tear himself away. When he got to his feet, he could feel a slight lightheadedness, not sufficient to compromise his balance, but enough to be aware that two drinks on an empty stomach had loosened slightly his grip on reality, and that he had to focus to avoid doing something foolish.

He thanked Marie as he made his way outside, and bid George farewell through the wound-down window of his car, glancing up at the man in a snapshot of contentment, surrounded by his cottage and garden, his world enveloped by the surrounding fields alive with bees, all shared with his wife and on the brink of a new business enterprise.

On a couple of the sharp bends in the narrow road away from the cottage, Spike found himself reacting a little more slowly than usual to the twists and turns, and he straightened himself up more in the seat. He turned the radio on, to focus his mind on the present rather than let it drift where it wanted, and as the pop music played his mind began to leave the cottage behind and focus on what lay ahead.

A lyric from one of the songs seemed to be repeated over and over again, like a mantra, with its message of conviction. "You can do it, Take your chance, Don't let the moment pass." As he reached the busier streets of Bartown, he reached into his pocket, steering with the other hand, and next to the notebook he felt the shiny surface of the pub's pepper pot. Not for the first time a phrase came to mind that suggested the outcome of what happened next would be taken out of his hands, that of 'Russian roulette'.

A car pulled out of a side turning right in front of him, forcing him to grab the wheel with both hands and stamp on the brake, firing a shower of loose road chippings noisily against the underside of his car from his skidding tyres. Instinctively he blasted his horn at the driver for his reckless behaviour, not caring if it led to an altercation. Only further along the road, as his pulse began to settled back to normal again, did he think that it had been a long time since he had vented his anger at another motorist by leaning on his horn.

The car park of the Horse & Barge was almost full. Just one space remained, but as he made his way towards it, another car, which had come in behind him but gone the opposite way around from the direction dictated by the arrows, nipped in first to secure the place. He had to drive back out and look for somewhere in the road, which meant a walk back along the pavement to the entrance, making his breathing a little more rapid as he hurried.

It was busy inside, but his two colleagues had secured a table, so he made his way to where they were seated, engrossed in an animated conversation. Carl was in full flow, regaling his new friend with a story, fuelled by the contents of a pint glass, which was now two-thirds empty.

Spike interrupted them long enough to find out what they were drinking, and then approached the bar, where Sapphire was serving. When his turn came, he asked her if she'd found the newspaper, as she dispensed the round of drinks.

"Yes. Sorry I didn't answer the door. I had a client with me," she said, which Spike had suspected already. "I'm around tonight if you want to try again," she said. It was what Spike had been hoping to hear, though at that moment tonight seemed a long way off.

"That'd be good," he said, asking for a menu as he ferried the drinks back to the table. Carl's story had just reached its climax, so Spike became the centre of attention as he took a seat with them, standing the menu up in the middle of the table.

"How was George Davison?" asked Harry.

"Entertaining," said Spike. "I could have talked to him all day. He gets calls from people with bees nesting in their attic and takes them away to one of his hives. He's been covered head to toe in them, after they left a lamp post and swarmed onto him, all twenty thousand of them clinging to his protective suit."

"It's probably his customers who are going to get stung now," said Carl "when they find out his prices."

"I don't think I'll mention how much he charges for his products. It seems to detract from the positive vibe of a new business start-up and the unusual things he's offering."

"Don't let the facts get in the way of a good story," said Harry. "Isn't that right, Carl?"

Carl was downing the remains of his earlier pint and moving the fresh one within easy reach. "I certainly would leave out any facts in a story that didn't fit the overall message. Why make things difficult for yourself by providing ammunition for someone who might disagree with what you're saying? Call it biased reporting if you like, but once you've made your mind up what you think, you make the facts fit that, to reinforce your argument."

"Anyone fancy something to eat?" said Spike, picking up the menu. He scanned the list and then passed it to the other two, who did the same, Carl with less enthusiasm than Harry, his favourite comestible being the liquid kind.

Spike offered to place the order for all of them, which he did with a different member of staff behind the bar, next to the door to the kitchen, paying for all three. She asked for his table number and then directed him to the self-service display of cutlery, serviettes and cruets.

Spike selected cutlery and serviettes for all of them and a salt cellar, all of which he managed to get in one hand. The other hand fumbled in his pocket for the matching pepper pot, which he had to rest on the surface while he removed the piece of tape over the holes. He glanced nervously across at the kitchen end of the bar, but the girl had gone, and then at Sapphire, but she was busy serving a customer. He picked up the pepper pot with his right hand and added the salt from his left, so that he could carry them together.

Carl was asking Harry what his plans were in Bartown, whether it was a stepping stone to greater things, as Spike placed what he had been carrying on the circular table in front of them. "In a year or two's time," Harry explained "if there's an opening that's a step up from here with a bigger salary, then maybe I'll have a look, but I'm already doing occasional weekend shifts down in London for the nationals, which pays well, with the chance of something full time down there if the opportunity comes my way."

"You fancy working in London full time?"

"If the right job on the right paper came along, why not? You've got to keep challenging yourself. A goldfish doesn't outgrow its bowl. You have to move it to a pond for it to get bigger."

When the food arrived, each helped themselves to cutlery and a serviette, leaving the pair of cruets as the only items in the middle of the table.

94

Carl took another swig of beer before sampling a chip from the edge of his plate. Harry armed himself with his knife and fork and began eating hungrily, slicing chunks of chicken and devouring them. Spike couldn't keep his eyes on his plate. Every time he put a forkful of food to his mouth, his eyes kept darting towards the other plates on the table and then at the untouched cruets, even though he tried not to let it happen. He picked up the salt cellar and sprinkled a little on his food, even though it was something that normally he would never do, replacing it alongside the pepper. But it didn't have the desired effect. Harry was working his way rapidly through his meal showing no signs of interest in the condiments, and Carl was still picking at his food with his fingers, almost eating under duress, like a child with a plate of greens that he has to eat to get a pudding.

A man's voice behind Spike said: "Are you finished with those?" and a hand pointed towards the two white ceramic pots in the middle of the table. Harry had just taken a mouthful of food but he muttered accession, leaning back a little to allow the neighbouring diner to reach over to pick them up. As he did so, another hand darted forward to grab them. Spike looked up and saw Sapphire lift them deftly from the table in one swift movement, while with the other hand she held out another set towards the diner.

"Here, have a fresh set," she said, which the man was happy to accept, returning to his table. "How are your meals?" she asked, to general nodding and positive noises. Spike had noticed that his hand was shaking. He let it hang down by his side as he looked up at her and found her looking straight at him. He watched her make her way back behind the bar and empty the two cruets into a tall plastic swing-top bin at the far end of the serving area, rinsing them under the tap used for washing glasses and stacking them upside down on a mesh surface to drain.

Harry finished his meal and began washing it down with the remains of his beer, running his tongue around the inside of his mouth to get a few bits of food from between his teeth. Carl had eaten about half of his, but his glass was empty, and he looked as if he needed another drink to tackle any more.

Harry glanced at his watch. "I've got a couple of people to see, so I'll have to cut and run, gents. What do I owe you?" he asked Spike.

"That's okay, Spike managed to say. It's on me." He was getting that cool feeling that comes when a moment of anxiety has just passed, like coming out of a visit to the dentist.

"I'll get the next one," promised Harry, and he made his way out, leaving Carl looking like a man in a desert. Spike took pity on him and bought him another drink, but didn't have one himself.

Spike watched him take a big swig out of his refilled glass. It always reminded him of when he'd once asked his colleague how he managed to drink so quickly, as if he had hollow legs. He'd said that it was on account of having had his tonsils removed, which meant that liquid could flow down his throat even more quickly than it had before. But the way in which he had said it had made it sound as if he'd had them removed for that specific purpose, not because of a throat infection. It had always coloured Spike's view of Carl, as if he were a man willing to go under the knife to remove any obstacle likely to come between his stomach and the amber liquid lined up in front of him awaiting its inevitable fate.

"How's the search going for your missing man?" asked Carl.

Spike had to admit to having run out of ideas. "The trail has gone cold. I know that something strange has been going on, but I can't find out what. The people I talk to fall into two categories: ones that are willing to talk but are just as puzzled as I am, and ones that know something but are keeping shtum."

Carl took another huge swig, smacking his lips in satisfaction. "Are you familiar with the works of Eliot?" he asked, somewhat randomly.

Spike searched his mind's 'filing cabinet' for anything in the folder marked 'Eliot'. "You mean The Waste Land and such." He knew he was on shaky ground when talking English Literature with Carl, who had a degree in the subject.

"I'm thinking of George Eliot, rather than T.S., journalist turned author of Middlemarch, Silas Marner and The Mill on the Floss. I was rereading her Mill on the Floss the other night and I happened across a line that jumped out at me, so I committed it to mind, which as you know I like to do. I offer it now for your edification." Carl paused for effect before delivering his bon mot. "It said: 'This is a puzzling world, and Old Harry's got a finger in it.'"

Carl took another long pull on his pint, leaving them both to ponder the potential appropriateness of the quotation, but Spike sought some clarification. "Is there a character in it called Old Harry?"

"That's the point," said Carl, cryptically. "There isn't. Old Harry is a nickname for the Devil." It left Spike wondering just how much Carl had observed of what had gone on with the pepper pot.

When they decided they had better get back to work, Spike allowed himself a glance towards the bar on their way out, but there was no sign of Sapphire. He wondered whether the invitation for tonight had been rescinded. He had hoped to see her face and get an indication of how things stood, but he didn't get the chance.

Chapter 17

Back in the office, Spike was facing the prospect of trying to write the beekeeper story while listening to Carl and trying to shake off post-lunch lethargy, but Tom came to his aid.

"Can you go round to St. John's churchyard? Apparently, there's a group of twitchers gathered there from all around the country because a woodchat shrike has been seen. Kat's already round there trying to get a picture."

There were times in his life when Spike felt the need to look skywards and say a thank-you, and this was definitely one of them. A nice, untaxing story and some fresh air; he would almost have done the job for nothing.

The vicar of St. John's was standing near the entrance to his church, enabling Spike to get a few details while observing the gaggle of camo-wearing bird-spotters and their battery of tripod-mounted lenses from a distance, one of whom was heading their way.

"I wouldn't know a woodchat shrike if it landed on my shoulder," admitted the vicar, looking across the headstones to the hedge at the far end of the graveyard. "But we could do with a bit of attention. There are more people standing in the corner of our grounds now than we get for most weekday services."

"You weren't tempted to get out the collection plate and charge for entry?" suggested Spike, to the amusement of the vicar.

"God's house is open to all-comers, whether it is the spiritual world or the natural world that brings them here. As long as they don't trample on the flowerbeds, they are welcome to spend some time here free of charge."

One of the group passed them on his way to his car, a tripod and viewing scope over his shoulder, having got the sighting that he wanted to be able to tick the species off on his list. Spike asked him how far he had come, and got the answer "Hemel Hempstead," in reply, but from the look of satisfaction he was wearing it had clearly been worthwhile. Spike got a few details and a quote from him as the vicar left to attend to his duties.

Spike found a seat in the churchyard from where he could count the heads in attendance, and soon saw Kat making her way towards him, a longer lens on her camera than she normally employed.

As she got near to him, she stopped and put down her long lens, which was attached to a monopod. She pointed a second camera around her neck towards him, taking a photo of Spike on the bench, surrounded by the long rows of gravestones.

She picked up her other lens and joined him on the seat, her face betraying a look of success. "A man in his element," she said, laying the expensive lens down between them. "Maybe you'll be here yourself one day."

"Did you bag your first woodchat shrike, then?" he asked.

"After a bit of a wait. Most of the time I could see only a tail or a wing behind the leaves, but it finally showed itself properly. I got some shots of the group in their anoraks with their equipment as well."

"Sounds like it's something that you're not going to take up full time?"

"A bit too much standing around for my liking. I prefer more action. What have you been up to since I last saw you?"

The question made Spike wince, though hopefully not visibly. "It's a long story."

"I thought stories were your bread and butter."

"So did I. Let's just say I didn't get my own back like I said I would when you asked before."

They both looked out across the graves. "Probably for the best. Revenge can leave a bad taste, and then come back to bite you."

"Yes," agreed Spike. "I sometimes think I'm being taught a lesson when things don't go as I'd planned." He thought about what he could have been facing if things had gone differently, one problem swapped for another. So often, it seemed, sobriety was accompanied by regret. "I'd better be getting back to the office," he said.

"You'll just have to find your missing man before anyone else does," she suggested as they got up to go, trying to sound encouraging, while handing him an envelope of images from a previous job to pass on to Tom, to save her a journey.

"Yes. And when I do, you'll be the first to know."

Spike was planning to dodge the office in favour of a writing session at home, but having the photos to deliver meant going back inside. He was pleased to find the reporters' room empty, and also no sign of Tom, who must have sent Carl out on a story and gone out on an errand himself. It felt like a bonus being able to work uninterrupted.

On his desk he noticed a note from Tom as he hung his jacket on the back of his chair. It was on top of a pile of handwritten WI reports, and the note asked him to type them out for next week's column.

As Spike was looking through his notebook and putting together the story on George Davison, his attention kept being drawn to the name on the top of the pile. It had been written by a Mrs Nesbit, a name that seemed familiar. He flicked through the earlier pages of his notebook and there it was, Mrs Nesbit, a member of the writers' group, which he'd written down in the library. Could that be the same Mrs Nesbit?

Spike fetched the dog-eared local phone book from the shelves against the wall and started looking through the Ns. There were two Nesbits, one with a single 't' and one with two. A habit he had picked up from his time as a reporter was always to check the spelling of any name he wrote down against the original before moving on, even if it was only a shopping list or a note for a colleague. Even when he knew there was no logical reason for making sure that he spelt Mothers Pride with no apostrophe, because that was how it was printed on the packaging, and no one would see his shopping list except him, he still had to write it correctly, it being a habit he couldn't break. Just occasionally, like now, it came in handy, a useful 'tic' to have in his personality. He felt sure that the writers' group member had a single 't' to her surname, because that is how he had written it down.

Unable to concentrate now on the beekeeper story until he had explored this lead, he rang the number and after a short wait heard a click and a woman's voice on the other end.

Spike introduced himself and said he was in the process of typing out her WI report, which he said was very interesting, and added how grateful the paper was for her contributions.

"I do try to make it as readable as I can," she replied, seemingly flattered by the compliment. "It's something I enjoy doing."

Was she, Spike wondered, the same Mrs Nesbit who was a leading light in the local writers' group? There was more than a trace of pride in her voice when she replied. "Yes. I'm surprised you know about us. We are only a small group."

"We try to keep in touch with what is happening in our local societies, no matter how small. We know what valuable work they do." Spike waited for the follow-up compliment to register, then added: "Do you know a Maureen Farrell from the writers' group?"

"Yes, she was a member for a while, but that's a few years ago now."

"I think she was friends with Geoffrey Fellows?" suggested Spike.

"Yes, they did rather hit it off. They both stopped coming at about the same time. I understand he's still missing. A sad business. I do hope they find him safe and well. A friend said perhaps he's lost his memory and is unaware where he is or how to get back home. You read about things like that happening. The irony is that many of our members would create a plot around something like that, but not Geoffrey. He preferred to write non-fiction. He wasn't given to flights of fancy. They do say that the quiet people are the ones you have to watch." Mrs Nesbit was enjoying having a member of the newspaper's staff on her phone, and began to digress. "I also help out with the town's amateur dramatics society, and we are always looking for some publicity. Do you know about us?"

Spike was on the back foot for a moment, having had his bluff called about his boast of keeping up to speed with even the smallest of groups. But then a thought occurred to him. "Did you have a production of a Tom Stoppard play?"

"Yes," said Mrs Nesbit, delighted at the recognition. "Did you see it?"

Spike had to think on his feet again. "I heard about it. Wasn't there a fake dead body on stage for a lot of the performance?"

"That's right," said Mrs Nesbit. "We had to raise the money to buy one. Very realistic it was, too."

Spike still had a vivid picture in his mind. "I can imagine."

"We are rehearsing for our next production at the moment. You must come along when it's on."

"What are you doing this time?" asked Spike.

"An Inspector Calls."

Spike sucked in his cheeks. "I'll try to find the time, but I'm not sure that detective stories are really my thing."

He thanked her for her help and for the information, and after replacing the phone he thought for a moment about what she had said about the two authors. It looked as if Colin Mears, the so-called rival, had painted a more accurate picture of Geoffrey Fellows than Maureen Farrell, judging by Mrs Nesbit's casting vote, and that affairs of the heart had something to do with it. Perhaps if she had been jilted by Geoffrey, she had adopted a less-than-generous opinion of him.

Spike glanced at the clock. If he knuckled down, he could get the beekeeper story written before driving out to Sapphire's flat to see whether he was still welcome. Soon he was fully immersed in the world of honey and mead production in his head, the old typewriter rattling out the words as they came to mind, with the quotes from his notebook to back up his descriptions.

He was sure that a corny headline would get placed above the words, since bees, hives and golden honey were a rich source of puns and allusions, though most readers were aware that reporters didn't write the words in large type that drew their attention to the story. That was left to sub-editors, many of them former reporters who'd had enough of the unpredictable hours and energetic nature of the work and swapped them for a pay rise and a desk job. What would they come up with, he mused, something along the lines of: 'New business was meant to bee'. Spike winced at the thought, but hoped that his words had done justice to George and Marie's endeavours. He wasn't sufficiently tired of reporting yet to join the ranks of the desk-bound.

He tucked his folded sheaf of folios in the drawer of his desk, remembering Harry Dixon's request for a few lines for the *Evening Post*. That could wait until tomorrow. Right now he needed to be elsewhere.

Spike's car's suspension complained as he bumped the wheels up over the kerb to reach the drive in front of the flats. It made him aware that he had done it a few times now. This time there was no woman picking a button to press next to the front door. Spike glanced up at the window as he walked towards the panel of doorbells. Once again, he wasn't sure whether or not there was a light in the background through the upper window.

After pressing the button, Spike waited for a few moments, but there was no answer. A feeling of disappointment came over him. He remembered how as a child he had sometimes been left waiting at the school gates, having been offered a lift home by one of his parents who had then forgotten and never came. The feeling of hope as another car came along the quiet road towards the school, followed by the sadness when it drove on past, would make a lump form in his throat as he stood there alone, unwanted.

There was still no answer to his press of the doorbell, so he went back to the car and had opened the door to get in to drive away when he heard the buzz that released the front door to let him in. He made his way quickly to the door, almost running in case the buzzer stopped. Had she been busy or just not sure whether she wanted to see him again, making up her mind as he stood below? But he was in, and for now that was all that mattered.

The door to her flat was open, and he closed it behind him, wiping his shoes on the small mat. He put his head around the door to the living room, and she was sitting in the familiar place, waiting for him, her face turned up towards him.

"I didn't know whether I was still welcome," he said, still only part way through the door from the hall.

"Everyone is welcome. I don't turn people away."

"You're the second person to tell me that today," he said, taking a seat in front of her. "The other was a vicar standing outside his church."

"Maybe we are in the same line of business."

"I ought to apologise for earlier, in the pub."

"Maybe it isn't me that you ought to apologise to. Maybe it's yourself."

"I can get a bit carried away sometimes. If I like someone or dislike someone, it's difficult not to do something about it. It just seems right at the time, though not afterwards. Then I regret it."

"Especially when the punishment doesn't fit the crime."

Spike nodded, shamefully. "How did you know, about the pepper pot?"

"You've got a bit of work to do on your conjuring skills. Besides, I heard the landlord the day before saying he couldn't believe what people would steal these days when he found that there was a pepper pot missing. What was in it?"

"Some seeds that I'd ground into a powder."

"Poisonous ones?"

"Supposedly."

She sighed, and for a moment there was silence between them. "There's a dark place in you," she said, finally. "But I can help you with that. I can make you stop wanting revenge."

Spike shifted uncomfortably in his seat. "I don't know if I'm ready for that."

"Because you want to stay angry or for some other reason?"

Spike didn't reply, so she continued. "There's something in your past that you don't want to face. You've locked it away, but you can feel it's still there. And you know that if you don't open it, it will always be there and always hurt, and when it hurts, you want others to suffer like you do."

Spike was beginning to wish that she hadn't pressed the buzzer to let him in. This wasn't what he had hoped to be doing. He had thought she might have admonished him, and then they would have moved on, but this was harder to bear.

"It was all a long time ago, too long to relive by explaining."

"The past is never too long ago to revisit," she said. "But you need to want to do it."

It was the first sign that she was accepting his refusal, for now. But he knew that she had prepared the way, and that she hoped when he was alone with his thoughts that he would reconsider.

"When you're ready," she said, finally. "I'll be here."

"Did you read the letters in the paper?" he asked, glad to change the subject.

"Yes. It was kind of people to write positive things. There's been a lot of interest since the article came out."

"Not enough to go full time, though?"

"It works well the way it is. I get to do something very different, and I get to observe people at the same time."

"You don't get too much of people, dealing with the public all the time?"

"I don't know if you can get too much of meeting people."

"I wish I could say the same."

"That sounds as if your job is making you feel that way. Maybe that's because a lot of what you report on is about suffering. The greater the suffering, the more interest it creates, but even other people's pain can become a burden in time."

It was an argument that Spike couldn't counter. There was a saying among news reporters that he had heard, that you could always tell who was the reporter at the scene of a disaster, because he or she would be the one smiling. There was no such thing as bad news, because the bigger the disaster the better the story. But he didn't want to dwell on the effects that a daily diet of bad news had on those who reported on it. "There was something I wanted to ask you," he said.

She had that look again, the one that seemed to be reading his thoughts. "Have you asked yourself why you want to ask it first?" she said.

"I'm trying not to, because I know it's just me wanting to be ahead of the crowd, but I have come to a bit of a dead end with the missing man case. I don't know how to move forward, and I know if I do nothing, someone will get there first."

"And that would matter?"

"Unfortunately, yes. I wish it didn't, but right now it does."

"That's your problem. You are so afraid of failure, you can't see that you already have the answer. You are concentrating so hard on not knowing what to do next that you have forgotten that you know already."

"I do?"

"Yes. If you stopped thinking that you don't know, you would realise that you do. When you can't remember someone's name, the harder you try, the further away it gets from you, because you are frustrated with yourself for not remembering. But as soon as you stop trying and let go of your frustration, you remember it straight away."

Spike looked as if he wanted to believe her, but he didn't know where to start, so she prompted him. "Does the name Susan mean anything to you?"

He rolled it around in his head for a moment, at first thinking of people he knew with that name, in his past, and then more recently, and a photograph came to mind, and an item of jewellery and a gathering at a Golden Wedding, and suddenly he realised. There was a loose end that he hadn't tied up. It was maybe nothing, but he had overlooked it.

"How did you know about that?" he asked.

"It was there, all the time, in your mind. I just brought it to the surface."

Spike smiled. He wanted to laugh, but he didn't want to offend her, though maybe she knew that's what he thought of doing anyway. He didn't know whether to believe her, like Captain Marvo, whose tricks in front of his eyes were too quick and clever to fathom, yet he knew that they couldn't really be magic, because magic doesn't exist, does it? Maybe she was right. Maybe he should stop trying to understand and start just going with what happened to him. Maybe that was the way forward, to question less and just ride the wave. He felt refreshed, unburdened even. "I really ought to start paying you for these visits," he said with a laugh. "I feel like a cheapskate getting your help for free."

"When you decide it's time to open your past, and I can really get to work, that's when you can pay me. Until then, this is just polite conversation. When you're willing to go under, that's when the real work begins."

Driving home through the quiet streets, Spike felt as if he were returning from a different planet. People wouldn't believe him if he tried to tell them where he had been, not that he would. It was too special and too personal to share it with those who might pour scorn upon it. It was enough that he had his own bubble of awe and wonder, and a place where he could go and find it again when he felt the need to replenish.

Chapter 18

Spike was in early the next day, his untouched car still an enjoyable novelty, to hand over his words on the beekeeper and knock out a few lines about the couple's new business to put on the van to the *Evening Post*. Then he gave Tom the envelope of photos from Kat and told him about Susan, the woman who made jewellery for friends.

Tom liked the sound if it and told him to take Kat with him to get some pictures of her with a selection of her creations. He had planned to ring her to arrange a visit, but a piece of advice came to mind from Spike's early days as a reporter. A news editor had taken him to one side, perhaps seeing some potential in him that made it worth the effort to pass on a lesson he had learned. It was that when you aren't sure whether to ring someone or just turn up at their door, always go for the doorstep option. He had learned how turning someone away when they were face to face was a lot harder than opting out on the phone. As this was Spike's last-chance lifeline to the missing man case, he knew he couldn't afford to let it become another dead end.

But he had only a Christian name. He took a copy of the local Yellow Pages down from the office shelves and found the section on jewellery. Alongside it was a category for jewellery makers with, surprisingly, several entries for the county.

One was for a Susan Riley, and when he compared the phone number listed against her name with the one in his notebook that she'd given him at the Golden Wedding, they matched.

He jotted down the address, and was aware that it was not that far from the Golden Wedding couple's home, where they had met. The photos in the envelope from Kat that he had given to Tom had turned out to be spares of the Golden Wedding shoot to pass on to the couple, so Spike offered to drop them in on his way. After a quick call to Kat he was on his way, hoping that the couple weren't late risers.

Bob Chivers was in his front garden clipping his shrubs when Spike's car drew up alongside. He recognised him as soon as he stepped out of the car, giving him a cheery wave as Spike walked around it to the front path. "You're the young fella from the newspaper," he declared. It was always nice to be remembered.

"We saw that bit you wrote, and the picture. It was lovely."

"I've got a few pictures for you, in case you want to get one framed." Spike held out the envelope and watched the old man's face light up as he viewed the enlargements.

"You'll come inside and have a cup of tea." Spike had planned to dodge the invite, but it was said with such certainty that he didn't have the heart to decline. Bob showed his wife the prints while he put the kettle on, and soon Spike was sitting on the edge of their sofa, sipping from the best china, a selection of home-made cakes on a stand next to him on a nest of tables.

"I'm on my way to see your friend, Susan Riley," he told them. "We'd like to do an article on her jewellery making."

"She'll be pleased about that," said Bob. "I think she needs something to cheer her up. She and her husband have split up. We didn't find out until after our Golden Wedding get-together. We felt guilty when we heard, celebrating our long marriage when hers was in trouble, but she kept it to herself at the time. I do hope they manage to patch it up. Sometimes it's only when you're apart that you realise what you miss."

After another cup of tea and a scone, Spike managed to extricate himself from the generous embrace of the Chivers, and headed to Kat's mother's house to collect her en route to Susan Riley's. He apologised for being later than he'd said, but when he told her that he had called at the Chivers to deliver her prints, she understood immediately how difficult it could sometimes be to detach oneself from the warn hug of gratitude.

"Did they like the pics?"

"I think it's safe to say that if you're ever passing, there'll be a plate of scones with your name on it."

Susan Riley's home was at the end of a long drive bordered by a tall hedge. There was a garage at the end of it, alongside a large house, which looked as if it would have at least four bedrooms, and a car, a blue Peugeot, parked on the drive close to the house. Spike had left his car in the main road and they had walked up to the front door.

It took a few moments for the door to be answered, but the face of the blonde woman who opened it was the one he recognised from the Golden Wedding. She looked surprised, at first unsure of who he was, but the sight of a camera around the neck of his accomplice reminded her of where she had seen them both before.

"Hello, Mrs Riley. I don't know if you remember, but we met at the Chivers' Golden Wedding party. I'm Spike, from the *Bartown Chronicle*. This is our photographer, Kat. We were in the area and I remembered that I'd mentioned about maybe doing an item for the paper on your jewellery making. I thought I'd see if it was convenient."

Susan Riley's face had gone through surprise and recognition to a suggestion of unease. Normally, Spike would have taken this as a warning that he might not get as much as he'd hoped from the interview, because it was an awkward time, but on this occasion, he knew that the element of surprise was key to his chances of success.

"Um… Right… Um… Well, you'd better come in then." It wasn't the welcome that either of them had wanted to received, but the important thing was that they were over the threshold and able to make her more at ease as she got used to the idea.

She led the way through to her living room, where she offered them seats, saying: "What would you like to know?"

"Have you got any examples of your work that we could photograph, to give our readers a taste of what you do?"

Susan opened the fold-down front of a cabinet, which looked like her work desk, and brought several items in boxes for them to see. Kat arranged them on the dining room table at the far side of the lounge, where there was natural light from a side window.

One of her specialities was fingerprint jewellery, using a particular kind of special clay to take an imprint of a child or a partner's finger, then engrave their name alongside and fire it in an oven to create a permanent silver trinket for a necklace, brooch or cufflinks.

Susan sat behind the examples that she had arranged with some of the tools that she used while Spike asked her about her work, how she had got into it and how she found her clients. As she added some engraving to an ornate gold brooch, she relaxed as she concentrated on the detailed work, forgetting that she was in the limelight. Spike remembered a photographer colleague once telling him that if the subject was at all nervous, he always got them to hold something familiar to them, and said that they became visibly more relaxed and able to conjure up a more natural smile with a prop in their hand.

What had started as a hobby for Susan had become a business, her client list expanding by word of mouth as past customers recommended her to their friends. Sometimes they wanted something specific, but at other times they asked her to create something for a particular anniversary or birthday, and left the choice of what to make to her.

She said she had always enjoyed working with her hands, from her schooldays, with handicrafts and later sewing and knitting. But what gave her satisfaction was the act of creating something; she felt that those who made things for a living were happier in themselves than those who didn't have anything tangible to show for their day's employment.

As she was putting the items back in the work desk, there was a noise from somewhere else in the house, followed soon after by a click, which sounded like an outer door closing. "My husband," she said, her back still towards them. "He's tidying up the back garden."

Spike looked at a line of family photos on the windowsill, the one in the middle being most likely of her husband. He was crouching on a lawn with their two dogs. Spike took a couple of steps towards it to get a closer look. "You don't have the dogs anymore?" he asked.

She turned to see where he was looking. "Oh, no. They became a bit too much to handle, so he gave them to a friend. He still sees them from time to time."

"What sort are they?" asked Spike.

"Um… Tosa."

"Is that the same as Japanese fighting dogs?" asked Spike.

"Yes. That's right. They were my husband's choice. He and his friend used to show them. They won a few prizes in local competitions. He used to say his dogs would do anything for him if he asked them, he even joked they'd kill for him. They were his life. He didn't want to give them up, but they became too much for me as they grew bigger. I couldn't live with them, so I told him it was them or me."

With her jewellery creations put away, she saw her visitors to the door. "Thanks for your time," Spike told her. "We can let you have a couple of pictures, if you'd like."

"Yes, that would be nice," she said, looking more relaxed now.

"Hopefully the article will bring you some extra business."

As they walked down the drive to the road, Spike said to Kat: "Are you in a hurry to get back?"

She shrugged. "Not particularly. Why?"

Instead of crossing the road to the car, Spike glanced behind them to check that they couldn't be seen from the house, and then looked along the other side of the hedge that bordered the drive. Instead of a house next door there was a long, narrow drive with a fence either side, most likely leading to a house set back from those close to the road.

"Have you got that long lens with you?" Kat unzipped a pouch on her camera bag and took it out. "Can you try getting a picture through the hedge to the back garden?" he asked. She gave him a quizzical look, but didn't question his motive.

Together they made their way quietly up the neighbouring drive, past Susan's garage, to a point where they were in line with the back garden. The closeboard fence had tall shrubs behind it, and for a moment it looked as if they wouldn't be able to see in. But Kat handed her camera to Spike, whispering: "Hold that for a moment," and with her hands on top of the fence she was able to pull herself up high enough to swing one leg and then the other on to the top and then down the other side, where there was still a line of tall vegetation between her and the garden.

Spike lowered the camera over the top by its strap until she had it on the other side, and then waited while she found a gap to push the lens through. There was silence for several minutes, and Spike found himself looking up and down the lane that was someone's drive, wondering what he would say if the owner came long. He kept silent, despite an urge to ask what was happening, and eventually he heard a couple of faint shutter noises as the camera was fired from further along the fence. Then he saw the camera being dangled over his side of the fence a little way from where he was standing, so he hurried down to where it was, whispering "Okay," as he took the weight of the camera and lens.

A couple of seconds later Kat's upper half appeared over the fens, followed by her legs to one side, and she jumped down onto the ground, dusting herself down, retrieving her camera bag and reclaiming her camera.

Spike couldn't resist whispering to her as they heading back towards the road. "What did you see?"

"There was a chap doing the garden, so I took a couple of shots of him. I don't think he saw me."

Back in the car they both sighed as the tension of the moment ebbed away. "I knew that karate training would come in handy for something," he told her, starting the car. "All that high kicking keeps you supple."

"Not quite what I expected to be doing when asked to photograph jewellery, but I suppose it's all in a day's work."

Back at her mother's home he asked if she would develop the film while he waited, and she let him watch the process of measuring chemicals and taking temperatures in the strange glow of weak yellow light that accompanied the alchemy, the bathroom door locked and a black velvet sheet hung over it to stop any stray light getting through.

The developed black-and-white film had to be hung up to dry, and then it could be cut into strips and placed in an enlarger to create an image on a sheet of photo paper. Using a pair of tongs, Kat agitated the paper in the tray of liquid and an image began to form. Spike peered at the paper, willing it to take shape before his eyes, his head just above the surface, his nostrils filled with the smell of the chemicals.

She moved it to a second tray to stop the process and then a third tray to fix the image, before cleaning it free of chemicals in water. The ripples on the surface as she agitated the paper prevented a clear view, though Spike could see there was a man crouching next to a flowerbed with a trowel in his hand. But a few seconds later Spike was able to get his first good view of it.

The face was side-on, not looking at the camera, and it made Spike's heart begin to race. It wasn't definitely the face he'd hoped for, but one thing was for certain, it wasn't Susan's husband.

Kat had a copy of the previous week's *Bartown Chronicle* in her kitchen showing the missing man, and Spike put it on the table alongside the still-damp print. "What d'you think?" he asked her, though she could tell from the uncertainty in his voice that he wasn't convinced. "Are they the same man?"

"I think you need a clearer picture," she told him.

"I can't write anything until I know, but I can't confront her without knowing who he is. Maybe she's got a brother who was also in the garden."

"I think my fence climbing days are not over."

"What d'you think the chances are of a picture that makes it clear once and for all?"

"I'd say the clearer the picture, the greater my chance of getting caught. And if it isn't your man, and it turns out to be all perfectly innocent, it could mean trouble for both of us."

Spike wanted to spare her any repercussions, since she was trying her best to help him. But he kept thinking how Susan had said it was her husband. If the thick-set man in the photo on the windowsill struggling to crouch on the lawn with the dogs was her husband, she was lying about the slim chap squatting with ease in the back garden. And why would she do that?

Kat knew the look that Spike was giving her. His mind was made up, he just couldn't phrase the words in a sympathetic way. Even a wordsmith could sometimes get flummoxed.

"I'll go back tomorrow and have another go," she said. "I've got a teleconverter attachment that I can fit on the lens to double the length. With a decent amount of light, I should be able to get a full frame of his face. And if he sees me and turns towards the camera, we'll have the picture you want, but also the hassle of justifying it."

Spike thanked her. "I wouldn't have asked if this whole story hadn't been riding on who that bloke is."

"I know," she said. "I didn't think you were doing it just to wind me up."

"I'll owe you big time if this comes off," he told her.

"I know that as well."

Chapter 19

It was lunchtime when Spike got back to the office, and so he had the reporters' room to himself. He called in at the bakery shop to get something to eat while he was working, and he recognised the figure being served in front of him as he walked through the door. As the owner of the garage turned to leave with his lunch, Spike said a cheery "Hello!"

The man looked up and smiled in recognition. "All right?" He paused for a moment, remembering why Spike had visited him recently. "How's your parking problem?"

"Gone away, it seems, thanks to you. I'm not sure how you did it, but I'm very grateful."

"Like the sign says: 'Miracles we can manage; the impossible may take a little longer.'"

"You can mend more than cars, it seems."

"All I did was oil the wheels a bit to make things happen. I'd better get back. Take care."

"You, too."

Spike munched on a sandwich from the bakery bag at his desk as he typed the story about Susan Riley, trying not to get mayonnaise on the keys of his typewriter.

All the time he was writing he thought about what she had said about her husband being in the back garden, and the picture of him that had been on the windowsill. When he'd finished the piece for the paper, he got one of the bound volumes of back issues from a few years ago off the shelf where they were stacked in rows in Tom's office, each one's spine showing the year in gold lettering.

Spike flicked through the yellowed pages, trying not to get distracted by the stories and familiar faces, but turning to the show results in each issue. The dog shows were held in the spring each year, so he was able to ignore whole chunks of each binder and concentrate his search where it was most likely to be successful. Sometimes there were just a couple of photos and a column of text, while in other years, perhaps in a slow news week, a whole page had been given over to a show, with categories such as the 'dog that looks most like its owner', which strangely named the owner as the winner, not the dog.

When he had worked his way through almost a decade of binders, fetching each one from the other office and leaning it on his typewriter keys while resting the foot of the pages on his lap, he told himself that he would look at just one more and then have a break. It was then that he saw a photo that made him drop the bunch of pages that he had already lifted in readiness to turn to the following week. Two men were photographed with a dog, holding a prize rosette and smiling. One was the same man as the one in the photo on Susan Riley's windowsill, holding the collar of a Japanese fighting dog, and the other man was Darren Rumsey.

For several minutes Spike stared at the page, engrossed. He didn't know why it made him feel slightly lightheaded, seeing this image, or even whether it was significant, but something told him that it would be. It felt as if it was confirmation that his suspicions were leading him along the right track.

The caption with the photo gave their names as Joe Riley and Darren Rumsey, and the category as Best Foreign Breed. Spike made a note of the date of the paper and the page number, closing the binder to return it to Tom's office.

As he was about to get up, the door to the reporters' room opened and Tom appeared, returning from lunch, asking how the jewellery woman story had gone. Spike handed him the words, telling him that the pictures were on their way, but keeping quiet about the man in the back garden until he knew more about his identity.

"I've had a call from the postman who tripped over the flowerpot," said Tom. "He read your piece in this week's paper about the legal costs and wants to talk to you about it."

Spike was always wary about readers wanting a word about a story he had written. "He's not annoyed about us talking to the flowerpot man, is he? I could do without another telling off over that story."

"He didn't sound angry on the phone. I think he wants to make a suggestion. Can you give him a ring and arrange a meeting?" He handed Spike a piece of paper with the name Reggie Patterson and a number scribbled on it.

There was a lengthy delay before anyone answered when Spike rang the number, and the man's voice sounded slightly out of breath. Spike introduced himself, and the man on the other end sounded pleased that he had called, apologising for the delay because his leg was in plaster and he was using crutches to get around. "I was interested in what you said about Appleby being fleeced by his solicitors," he explained. "It looks like costing me an arm and a leg… well, a leg anyway… and I've been warned that even if I win, I'll lose most of the money to the legal people, so I won't end up any better off. With us both in the same boat, I wondered if you could act as a peacemaker or a go-between to get us together to call it off? There would be a story in it for you."

Spike was glad that it wasn't a complaint about what he had written, and warmed to the idea of a truce.

"Where do you want to meet, if he's agreeable to it? Somewhere neutral perhaps?"

"Maybe a pub in town. We could have a drink to seal it and you'd get your picture."

Spike already had a venue in mind. "Do you know the Horse & Barge?"

"Yes, it used to be on my round a few years back."

"I'll get in touch with Charles Appleby and let you know what he says. If he's up for it, would tomorrow lunchtime be okay?"

The man with the plaster cast agreed, so Spike phoned the other party in the arrangement to run the proposal past him.

Charles Appleby sounded a little surprised, and also slightly wary, but he seemed to be coming round to the idea the more he thought about it and eventually agreed to the meeting.

As Spike was confirming the arrangements with the postman, Carl had returned from lunch, his swagger suggesting that it had involved the intake of liquid.

"You getting your warring factions together to bury the hatchet?" he asked.

"Hopefully," said Spike.

"They'll be calling you Bartown's answer to Henry Kissinger if it comes off. Next job the Middle East."

"It makes sense instead of them both being out of pocket. The only winners in these sorts of cases are the lawyers."

"Make sure you have them both frisked before they meet. You don't want one of them pulling out a weapon and doing the other one in."

"I think they're both a bit more civilised than that. Besides, they've got only three legs between them, so if there's a fight, I don't think it will take much to pull them apart."

While he was talking, Spike had wandered across to where the office diary was kept open on a table, showing the week's jobs. He wrote in the following day's space 'Postman/flowerpot man truce – Horse & Barge' and his initials against it. He glanced at the other entries for the same day and saw that in the morning there was a 'New school gymnasium opening – Saint Theresa's'. There was no name against it allocating it to anyone, so Spike approached Tom, who was typing in his office.

"Is anyone lined up for this school gym opening tomorrow morning?" he asked.

Tom looked up from his keyboard. "Are you volunteering?"

"I could do with talking to someone there; it might be a way in while they're looking for publicity."

"Feel free." Spike added his initials to the diary. He took the folded copy of the college photo from between the pages of his notebook and took another look along the rows of faces as he rocked back on the hind legs of his chair, his feet resting on the desk's wooden foot rail. Was he looking at a young Jake Cousins, or was the former man with no name telling the truth about his school? It would certainly eliminate him from the missing man case if Geoffrey Fellows hadn't been one of his teachers.

The door to the reporters' room swung open and Harry Dixon appeared, crossing the room to his desk with a cheery "Hello, each!" Spike refolded the photocopy and put it back in his pocket. Carl looked pleased to see him, giving him an excuse to be distracted from his work. "All right, Harry. What's been going on?"

"I'm on the trail of the town's mayor. Seems as if he may have been getting a bit too friendly with one of his staff. There's a suggestion of inappropriate conduct and wandering hands." He crossed to where the *Bartown Chronicle*'s diary was displayed and he looked at the following day's entry. "He's keeping his head down, but he's supposed to be opening a school gym tomorrow, so I might just wander along to see if he shows up. If we have a snapper there at least we'll get a picture of him, maybe in his full regalia."

He noticed Spike's initials against the job. "Might be a livelier session than you'd expected," Harry told him. "A bit more interesting than a speech on the benefits to youngsters of PE lessons."

"Sounds as if he's been handing out lessons in physical education himself," joked Carl. "He did say in his last election leaflet that he had a hands-on approach to local government affairs, and that he was someone who liked to roll his sleeves up and get stuck in."

"You haven't still got that flyer, have you?" asked Harry, laughing at the appropriateness of the comments.

"I might have, somewhere," Carl told him, taking a deep breath before tackling the mound of loose papers covering almost the entire surface of his desk.

"It's always great to throw people's words back in their face when they screw up, especially if there are a few double-entendres among them to embarrass them even more."

As Carl hunted through the morass of discarded paperwork spread across his desk, Harry looked at the other entries in the diary. "Your postman wants to call off his legal action, does he?" he asked Spike. "That's a shame. I thought their fight through the courts might have made a good yarn." He flicked through a few more pages of the diary before returning to his seat.

"Here it is," announced Carl, brandishing a coloured, glossy leaflet issued by the mayor's office. "'My team and I will work tirelessly to provide a range of services in the local community,'" read Carl. "Maybe you should ask him if he's willing to bend over backwards to get things done." He waved the piece of paper towards a grateful Harry, who smiled as he read through it and tucked it into his notebook. "Much obliged." He looked at his watch. "I'd better shoot. See you gents tomorrow." The sheets of paper in the various trays on top of the filing cabinets that he passed on his way out lifted gently and dropped to their original position in salute on the draught created by his exit.

The gym at Saint Theresa's was a separate building from the school, a short walk away down a set of steps to a piece of land on a lower level than the playground. Spike was allowed a quick look around ahead of the official opening, and it reminded him of his school days.

There were all those items that were found nowhere else, such as wall bars, vaulting horses, long, low benches with pairs of hinged flaps at either end to hook onto other apparatus, and horizontal beams that could be lifted or dropped to the required height using a pulley rope. Long ropes hung like curtains from a track in the ceiling, and in the corner a container of footballs, medicine balls and bean bags awaited their first users, alongside an array of rubber mats.

Spike was introduced to the headmaster by his secretary, and he proudly provided all the figures on how long it had taken to build and how much it had cost, while supplying the necessary quotes on what an improvement it was on what they'd had before and how the pupils would benefit greatly.

While he had the headmaster's ear, Spike asked if he could get the secretary to check on the dates when a particular past pupil had attended the school, and the man in charge asked her to arrange that when the opening ceremony was over.

Not long after, a shiny black Daimler purred into the playground and, flanked by groups of children marshaled by their teachers, a balding man in a smart suit and hefty gold chain of office stepped out of the car and made his way to the entrance, where a purple ribbon had been fixed across the doors.

The town's mayor was handed a large pair of scissors and he did the honours with the customary declaration as he snipped the ribbon in two with a flourish.

Spike looked around for Harry Dixon and his photographer, but there was no sign of either. As the assembled crowd made their way into the gym, the secretary caught his eye and led the way back to her office to carry out his search request, allowing him to escape the post-opening gathering.

Her office was across the hall from the entrance to the school, and on the way there she confided that she was happy to go back to work and leave them to their socialising.

"What was the name of the person you wanted to check on?"

"Jake Cousins, or possibly Jacob."

She took down a box file from a set of shelves and then put it back and took down another. When she did the same with a third, Spike had an inkling of what was coming.

"Are you sure that was the correct name? We don't have anyone listed by the name of Jake Cousins as having attended."

"Maybe I'm wrong in thinking that he came here," said Spike. "It could be that it was another school entirely." He thanked her for her time, and said he hoped that the pupils enjoyed their new gym.

"They've been watching it come together for a long time," she said. "They're very excited now that it's finally finished. It was good of the mayor to make time to visit us."

At the Horse & Barge, Spike had arranged for an area to be set aside for the reconciliation, where a photo could be taken without the distraction of a backdrop of lunchtime drinkers. He had arranged for Kat to be there, and had been given permission to buy drinks on expenses to toast the truce.

Sapphire showed him the reserved table, in the corner at the end of the bar, giving Spike a look that seemed to him to suggest he behave himself this time, before returning to her customers. Then Spike recognised Charles Appleby, standing just inside the entrance looking around for someone he knew. He steered him towards the table and chatted to him while they waited for his postman, both trying to look relaxed despite apprehensions at the strangeness of the situation.

Spike had glanced at his watch for a third time when he saw a figure in the entrance to the pub leaning on crutches. He was making his way falteringly across the carpeted floor, a large plaster cast on his foot, when Spike intercepted him. Spike pointed towards Charles Appleby seated at the reserved table, and together they made their way to where he was waiting.

There was an awkward moment when neither party could think of the right words by way of a greeting. Asking 'How are you?' was hardly appropriate when you were the cause of the broken leg afflicting your fellow guest, and neither felt obliged to say: 'Pleased to meet you.'

In the end they settled for an exchange of 'Hello!' though without a handshake. The postman propped his crutches against the wall behind, and Spike left them together for a few moments while he ordered their drinks.

He hoped that the alcohol would improve their mood, and as they relaxed in the convivial surroundings, he waited for an improvement in their levels of bonhomie, then set about getting quotes to explain why they had taken the decision to settle their differences.

"I don't see much point in lining someone else's pockets when there's another way of settling this," said the postman. Charles Appleby nodded in agreement, doubtless holding back from saying that he hadn't wanted to get legal advisors involved from the outset.

Kat appeared alongside them, camera in hand, and Spike introduced her. She arranged the pair in a photogenic way, the postman's plaster cast and crutches displayed in the foreground of the shot, with glasses being clinked. She also got Charles to sign the cast for an alternative shot, though in neither picture did she manage to get the postman to smile, despite her professional banter and artful cajoling with her finger poised on the shutter release ready for the face to crease into a reluctant grin.

With her job done, she took an envelope out of her camera bag and handed it to Spike. "Here's something for you," she said, smiling in a way she'd hoped the postman had done. "I went back to that lane alongside the back garden and got a better photo this morning," she said. "I think it's what you were looking for."

Spike opened the envelope and shook the print out onto the bar, leaving his two guests for a moment. With Kat at his elbow, he focused on the picture, this time full face, and Spike knew as soon as he saw it that he'd found his man. He wanted to hug her, but it seemed inappropriate in that situation, and he could see from her face that she knew what she'd done.

With Kat on her way, Spike wanted to wind up the reconciliation, though he knew that these things took time. He was used to dipping in and out of moments, getting the details that he needed and leaving the parties to their Golden Wedding or gymnasium opening while he made his excuses and left. But after buying another round of drinks for his guests, he felt that he had reached a point whereby he could withdraw gracefully, citing work commitments as his need to be elsewhere. However, it was the postman who ended the meeting. After a visit to the loo, he didn't make his way to his seat, but stood beside the table, maybe not wanting the hassle of sitting down and having to get up again, having decided he would be on his way.

So, with a final polite exchange, they made their way out, everybody having achieved what they'd set out to do, the men having sealed their agreement to move on, and Spike having got his story and avoided any unpleasant confrontation of the sort that had been at the back of his mind.

It was in the office that Spike allowed himself another look at the photo in the envelope, having made sure that Harry Dixon wasn't hiding somewhere out of sight. Carl was keen to know whether the man with the cast had got plastered, informing Spike that: "Blessed are the peacemakers: for they shall be called the children of God."

Spike squinted at the face on the photo, comparing it with the one on the front of the previous week's paper, and felt a rush of excitement. He should have been writing the reconciliation story, but he couldn't wait to go back to Susan Riley's house and find out the truth. He could write the other story at home later, where there were fewer distractions.

The avenue that linked the drives and front gardens of the houses looked the same as it had the day before, but what had changed was Spike's mood, which he could feel building towards a sense of exhilaration the closer he got to the house. There was a line of parked cars on the other side of the road from the driveway, as before, but when Spike parked in the nearest available space to the house, he heard a car engine and saw the same blue Peugeot that had been parked in the drive coming out.

It turned away from him, heading away from town, and in the driving seat was Susan Riley, the passenger seat next to her empty. Spike waited for it to go out of sight before reaching for the door handle to get out and walk up the drive, but as he was about to open the car door, he saw a figure get out of one of the parked cars between him and the drive.

As the man turned to shut the car door, Spike was able to see his face. He recognised it from the photo on the windowsill as Susan Riley's husband.

116

Spike let go of the door handle and slid down in his seat, hoping he hadn't been seen. The man crossed the road and went up the driveway of Susan's house, walking with the purposeful gait of someone who belonged there.

Spike weighed up what to do. Should he go in as well and confront the two men? But neither of them had met him before. It would be better with Susan there. He decided to wait. Perhaps she had only nipped out to the shops and would return soon. He had waited a long time for this moment; he could be patient for a little while longer.

It was several minutes later, as Spike tried to imagine the scene inside the house, when Susan's husband walked back out of the drive to his car, this time in a more hurried fashion, and got inside, starting the engine.

Now what should he do? There was no time for weighing up the alternatives. He had to stay or follow. As the car came past him, Spike slid still further down in his seat, but popped back up immediately after and started his car. If he found out where Susan's husband was staying, he would have another line of enquiry to explore when trying to find out what had been going on.

By the time he had turned his car around, the one he was following was almost out of sight, but as he rushed to catch it up, he saw the brake lights come on and then it pulled over next to the kerb.

The engine was still running when the driver got out to use a phone box that he had stopped alongside, and after a minute or so made his way back to his car. But as he opened the door he glanced back along the road towards Susan's, where Spike was in his car just a little way up the road.

Spike couldn't be sure whether he had been spotted, but he waited as long as he dared before following, hoping that he wouldn't lose the car when the traffic got busier closer to town, which is where the car seemed to be heading.

It was about half a mile from the centre of Bartown when the car pulled over in front of a parade of shops, at the end of which was a small hotel. Spike looked for a space to park, but the only one was a little too close to his target for his liking. But it was either that or drive past and risk losing him, so he took a risk, trying to look absorbed in the parking manoeuvre and oblivious to the man locking his car door a little way in front.

Looking out of the corner of his eye, Spike saw him walk away from the car, and when he allowed himself a full view of what was happening, he saw the man heading towards the hotel entrance.

Spike got out and stood by his car for a moment, waiting for him to go inside, before striding along the pavement toward the hotel after him. The lobby was dark, and it took a moment for Spike's eyes to adjust to the gloom after the brightness of the street. As they did so and he was able to look around, he saw the man he was following standing next to a large and rather ornate fireplace and facing towards him, hands on hips.

Spike stopped, unsure whether to keep moving forwards or turn and leave, having at least learnt the man's destination. The man took a couple of steps towards him, a slight smile playing on his lips.

"Are you following me?" he demanded to know. Spike weighed up his options — 'Yes?' 'No?' Say nothing? In the end it was the last of these that became his choice, because the man didn't wait for a reply. "What time is it?" he asked.

Spike was momentarily stunned. Here he was in a strange hotel with a man he was pursuing and he was being asked by him for the time of day. He glanced up at the wall above the fireplace and found the perfect answer to the request. He pointed at the large clock on the wall, with its swaying pendulum and prominent numbers arranged around the face like the points of a compass.

The man half turned, as if merely to acknowledge Spike's discovery, not as if he were noticing it for the first time or indeed to note the unknown time. "Three thirty," he said, still with that unsettling smile. It was then that Spike realised what was happening, and as he did so a shiver went through his body. The clock, the smile the request for the right time. That was when he knew he had to go. He had fallen into a trap. He had been lured away to provide the object of his pursuit with an alibi, and the phone call on the way there had been to tell someone that the coast was clear to do whatever had been arranged.

Without a word he ducked out of the hotel and back onto the street, running back to his car and fumbling with the lock, his key not wanting to fit the first time of trying. As he pulled out into the road and made a U-turn to go back the way he had come, he glanced across at the hotel and saw the man he had just faced standing in the entrance, still grinning, but making no effort to follow.

There was an eerie calm at Susan Riley's house. Spike had hoped that there would be some sign of activity, maybe her car in the drive to show that she had returned, or someone going into the house or coming out of it, but instead there was just silence, broken only by the song of a bird.

Spike walked briskly up the drive, but he had taken only a few steps towards the front door when he saw what he had dreaded. It was open, and then, as he got closer, he could see the front mat hanging over the edge of the step, sideways to the door, as if it had been disturbed by a scuffle.

Stepping over it he crossed the threshold and walked slowly along the hall, aware that he didn't have permission to be there, but also aware that something had happened to make doing so essential. He felt a breeze on his face, and as he looked into the kitchen, at the back of the house, he saw that the back door was open, and close by a pedal bin had been knocked over.

He walked out into the back garden, seeing for the first time the area where Kat had been pointing her lens. There was a sun lounger on the grass, tipped on its side, and a book nearby, the bookmark a foot or so away from it, and a half-finished drink in a glass.

Spike looked up and down the garden, but he knew he was too late. Whatever had happened had taken place while he had been at the hotel, and now there was nothing left to see. He went back out to his car, looking up and down the road for possible clues, but there was none. Everything looked normal, except that what he'd had almost in his grasp had been snatched away.

Such was Spike's desperate sense of disappointment that he sought solace from an unlikely source. He needed to tell someone what had happened, and so even as he questioned the wisdom of his actions, he went back into the office to confide in Carl. At least a fellow reporter would understand the misery of having come so close only to be left with nothing.

As he explained what had happened to Carl over coffee laced with whisky, he at least had an attentive audience for the duration of the telling of the tale. But sympathy, that was perhaps asking too much, especially that late in the afternoon, when a combination of liquid refreshment and the prospect of going home soon brought out the playful side of the fellow reporter's character.

Carl chuckled to himself. "To misquote the great Oscar Wilde: 'To lose one missing man may be regarded as a misfortune; to lose him again looks like carelessness.'"

Spike should have known better, but his colleague hadn't finished. "I can see the headline now: 'Missing man gone again!' It's like when there was an election for a new pontiff and the new one didn't live for long, prompting the headline: 'Pope dies again!'"

He looked at Spike's disconsolate figure and reined in the humour. "You could always go to the police," he suggested.

"Yeah, right," Spike said sarcastically. "I've found your missing man, only I've lost him again."

"They may know already, if the jewellery woman has reported him missing."

Spike considered the likelihood, but he didn't think it stood up. "So, she's really going to ask for their help in finding him, having ignored all their appeals for anyone who has seen him to come forward for days, making their job more difficult than it would have been. I don't think so. I think she'll sit tight and wait to see what happens, and she won't want me nosing around."

"So where does that leave you?" asked Carl.

"Her husband is behind all this. I'm going to go back to the hotel and see if he's still around." It was late in the afternoon, and he knew that Carl would be heading home soon. But even so Spike said: "Keep this under your hat, would you? I don't want Harry Dixon hearing about it." Saying the name reminded him of his absence earlier at the school. "Has he been around today? He didn't appear at the opening of the school gym." Even as he said it, he realised that he had invited the old 'Am I my brother's keeper?' routine again, but for once Carl resisted the temptation.

"The word from my mate in head office is that he was told the mayor story was off limits. Turns out our mayor is a friend of the owner of our newspaper group, so even if Harry had got the story, it wouldn't have got published."

Spike winced. "And we criticise other countries for interference in the free press." As he mulled over the piece of information, he wondered whom Carl knew among the decision makers. "How did you hear that?"

Carl was smiling again, having been hoping that Spike would ask him that. "I couldn't possibly tell you," he said theatrically. "A journalist never reveals his sources."

Spike tried to counter his argument. "Not even to a fellow journalist?"

But Carl was ready for him. "Especially not to a fellow journalist!"

People were heading home from their offices and the shops when Spike parked in the road in front of the hotel. There was a familiarity about the action of locking his car door and walking towards the entrance, having done so just a short time before. It reminded him of something that a member of the public had once said to him when something had happened to them twice. "It's déjà vu," they had said, "all over again!"

It always made him smile inside, but now he needed to concentrate to avoid missing anything. This time there was a member of staff at the reception desk, unlike before, dressed in a smart uniform. The woman looked up at him in a welcoming way as he approached. "I'm here to see a Mr Riley. Can you tell me what room he is staying in?"

The receptionist continued looking at him for a second or two longer than he would have expected, before consulting the register in front of her. Was it his imagination, or was she checking him out before passing on any information? She flicked over the page, and then back again almost immediately after. "We don't have anyone of that name staying with us at present," she told him, her look polite but unwavering.

"You're sure?" he asked, but she didn't even look back down at the book. It was a pointless question, and her gaze confirmed it as such. She might easily have added: 'When I say something, I always mean it,' but politeness prevented her from doing so.

Spike turned to look at the clock above the fireplace on the opposite wall, as if the man he wanted to see might appear where he had last been visible. He thought about describing the man to her, in the hope that she would recognise him, but one look back at her face told him that she was not the sort of person to engage in a game of charades. He had been given the benefit of the doubt on an issue of security by allowing him to ask a question about one of their guests, but that was before he had supplied the wrong name, and now he was firmly in the 'suspect persons' category, to whom no quarter would be given lest they were indeed up to no good.

Spike wondered whether saying that in that case he would wait might earn him some sympathetic assistance, but he knew that if he employed that tactic, he would have to see it through, and he didn't fancy standing in the hotel foyer, under the constant scrutiny of the receptionist with the scraped-back hair, expecting him to make a bolt for the stairs at any second, like a security guard watching a would-be shoplifter. So, he settled for: "Maybe I'll try a bit later," which at least allowed him to save face, albeit only semi-convincingly.

Out on the street, he looked up and down the pavement, but none of the people hurrying by was the one he wanted to see. In the end he got back into his car and drove to the office. Carl would no doubt be on his way home now and he could write the school gym story in peace, he hoped.

As he was parking his car in the street outside, a familiar figure was coming the other way, up towards the entrance to the office. It was Kat, and she had an A4 envelope in her hand. They reached the steps at around the same time, both cheered by the synchronicity.

"You've saved me a walk," she said. "I was just going to put these on your desk. I'm meeting some friends in town and I'm late already."

She handed Spike the envelope. "Are these from the Horse & Barge job this morning?"

"Yes, and an extra one I put in. I didn't get the chance to say in the pub when I gave you the pictures from the back garden job, but I saw something familiar there. In the road outside the house there was a grey van, and I was almost sure I recognised it, so I took a picture. When I looked at it again in the darkroom I realised where I'd seen it. That guy with the dogs that I photographed chasing you outside the court a while back, I'm almost sure it's the same one."

Spike slid the photos out of the envelope and flicked through the pub pictures to the one of the van, the numberplate clearly visible in the photo.

"I'd better go or my friends will think I've stood them up," she said, glancing at her watch and making to move away.

Spike was momentarily stunned. He stared at the picture, before what she had just said registered and he shook himself out of his maze. "Wow!" he said. "I think that's another big favour I owe you," he managed to say, aware at the same time of the inadequacy of his words.

She could tell that her efforts held significance for him. "Put it on the bill," she said over her shoulder, skipping off along the street to make up for lost time.

In the office, Spike had a closer look at the photos, in particular the one of the van. He opened his notebook at the note he had made of the page number and issue date of the item in the binders. Pulling the right volume off the shelf in Tom's office, he opened it at the page he needed and took a look at the picture again of the two men with the dog and the rosette.

Struggling to hold the heavy broadsheet binder, he crossed the room to the photocopier and printed an image of the page, closing his eyes as the bright light shone through the gap between the hard-backed cover of the volume and the lid of the machine. The first effort didn't show the whole of the picture, so he moved the binder a couple of inches and pressed the button again, doing the same with his eyes again as the light traveled the length of the page and then back again.

Satisfied with his efforts this time, he replaced the volume on the shelves and sat at his desk, the photo of the van on the desk top and the photocopy propped up on the keyboard of his typewriter. He stroked his chin in a way that he found felt helpful when he had a problem to ponder. "What have you two been up to?" he asked out loud, as if they were able to answer, but neither replied.

He was about to turn his attention to writing the school gym story when the door to the reporters' room swung open and there was Harry Dixon. He crossed the room to his desk, in front of Spike, with a cheery: "Working late tonight?"

Spike managed to get the photos back in their envelope quickly without looking as if he were hiding something, followed by the photocopy. "Just writing the school gym story, but I think I've had enough. I'll finish it at home. I didn't see you at the school."

If Harry had hoped to avoid the question, he showed no sign of being thrown by it. "Something came up at the last minute and I had to be elsewhere," he replied, a downbeat tone to his voice, as if it were of no importance.

Spike made his way towards the door, envelope in hand. "You didn't miss much. When you've seen one mayor with wandering hands open a new school gym, you've seen them all." It was only when he was driving home that he remembered he had left the reject photocopy of the dog show men in the copier's tray back in the office.

Chapter 20

There were certain things that you could rely on when it came to your colleagues, Spike had discovered, and one of them was their timekeeping. Just as Carl would always be the last to arrive in the morning, wishing he could be elsewhere, Tom was always first.

Spike put it down to the weight of responsibility for all those empty pages that had to be filled with words every week, come what may, it was enough to make anyone start each working day early, lest the deadline of press day come around and the insatiable monster that was the *Bartown Chronicle*, which swallowed stories by the score, was still hungry for more.

Further down the pecking order there were fewer ulcers than higher up the ladder among the people paid to worry. Spike's job came with a willingness to work at any hour of the day, or night if needed, but when the story was typed, the weight was lifted. It was easier to sleep at night when you were on the bottom rung, mostly.

When he came into the office the following morning, before the front of house staff had arrived, it was with his stories written from the day before and a request in mind. On his way into Tom's office, he stopped to look at the diary on the table beside the window, and noted that he wasn't lined up for any arranged events for the next forty-eight hours.

He handed Tom the typed folios of the school gym story and the flowerpot man truce before he posed his question. He'd always found it wise to precede a request with the handing over of something that the recipient would find welcome, to foster an air of generosity. "If there's nothing pressing to be done for the next day or two, can I take a couple of days holiday?"

Spike was aware that the word 'holiday' probably sent a small shiver down the spine of his boss, given that it meant fewer hands contributing copy, but he also knew that arriving early on what would be a day off, armed with a couple of stories written in his spare time, would probably be enough to swing the request in his favour. "I've checked the diary," he added, hopefully, anticipating the question.

"I don't see why not," Tom told him, unfolding the pages of words that he had just been given. "Going somewhere special?"

"No, just staying local. I've got a few things that I want to sort out and now seems like a good time." As he passed the photocopier on his way out, he glanced at the tray to check that his reject sheet of paper was still there from the evening before, but it wasn't. All the more reason to devote himself full time to the missing man case and find out what had happened before someone else did.

It was strange leaving the office for the day before the town was fully awake, many of the shops yet to open, but that was how Spike had planned it. The reality matched the image he had formed in his head of how his day would begin.

The baker's shop was open, catering for a few early risers, so he stocked up with food and drink to last him a few hours, exchanging a few pleasantries with Mrs Pillsbury, for whom early mornings were a way of life, and bought a daily paper from the newsagent's next door.

Then he drove to a spot on a housing estate where he had parked before, and settled himself in for a wait. He had hoped that the grey van belonging to the occupant of the house would be parked outside, so he was disappointed to see it missing, but there were advantages in being in place before someone you were planning to follow had arrived, since it meant less chance of being observed.

Looking along the row of houses to the garden where he had stood at the gate, Spike recalled the confrontation with the two dogs guarding their territory. He was glad he was safely encased in a metal shell this time, though he knew if things progressed the way he wanted, that would need to end.

Every time he heard the sound of a car or van coming towards him along the quiet residential road he slid down in the driver's seat, but every time it was a false alarm. The smell of the sandwiches got the better of him after a while, and he allowed himself to be distracted by the newspaper, glancing up between stories to look for movement in the front garden, though he knew it was the van that would make things happen.

He may even have begun to doze a little in the warm sunshine coming through the windscreen, not enough to fall asleep properly and lose his awareness of time and place in a dream, but enough to be conscious of a slippage of time. It was during one of these 'cat naps' that he heard a tap on the window next to the kerb.

Opening his eyes suddenly he saw a face peering in the passenger's side window. For a second he thought it could be the man with the dogs, but as his eyes focused, he could see that it was an older man, a pensioner, and the expression on his face was one of concern.

"Are you alright?" he asked. The face was sharp and jutting and the eyes carried a sense of alarm, perhaps at what could be a potential emergency.

"I'm fine," Spike replied, trying to sound as normal as he could.

The man didn't look convinced. "It's just that you've been sitting out here for a long while." The face at the window wasn't accepting Spike's reassurance as sufficient explanation. He detected in the man's voice a trace of annoyance, wanting to get rid of him so that he could go back to his daily routine and relax. Spike knew that it was a short step from concern to a phone call to the police and the arrival of a car with a couple of officers demanding to know what he was doing. As he looked at the lined face, which must have seen its share of unpleasant things in its time, he knew that he would have to move. If the man with the dogs appeared now, he would be sure to be noticed.

"I was just about to go," Spike told him, and began tidying up around him with a view to moving. He knew that the pensioner had probably taken down his car registration, but if he left him alone now, he would probably be satisfied.

The man stepped back from the car, as if it were about to pull away, perhaps to encourage the driver to do so, but stayed in line with the window, to keep the pressure on to get the driver to move. "Thanks for your concern," Spike added with what he hoped was more than a trace of sarcasm.

As he started the car and drove slowly along the quiet road, he looked in his rear-view mirror as the man watched him go. 'Who needs neighbourhood watch teams,' thought Spike 'when you've got nosy pensioners with nothing better to do than twitch their curtains?'

Perhaps it was for the best, he told himself. He had been waiting there for a long time, certainly long enough. A phrase came to him from advice he had once been given, about not waiting for things to happening but making them happen. Be proactive. He knew that driving around aimlessly wasn't the answer. Something could be happening right now and he would be missing it, but he would be unlikely to stumble across it driving around at random. There would be no point in going back to Susan Riley's house, where the missing man had come from, nor to the missing man's wife's house, since he seemed to have been taken against his will, not returned to his former life to start again.

He didn't know where to find Susan Riley's husband, and the man with the dogs wasn't at home. That left only one loose end to investigate, that of Jake Cousins, who seemed to have lied about his school. If he turned up at his doorstep and asked if he could have a word, he could find out why he wasn't on the school register. The worst that could happen is that he would get turned away, which could indicate that something, or someone, was inside his flat that he didn't want anyone to know about.

As Spike turned the corner into the street where Jake lived, he stamped on the brake abruptly and pulled over to the side of the road, causing the car behind him to swerve around him. Up ahead, outside the flat, was the grey van that he had been looking for.

Spike felt his heart racing, banging in his ears. Having pictured the van returning to the house so many times that morning as he had waited outside, it made his throat go dry to finally see it in front of him. He manoeuvred his car closer to the kerb, to avoid standing out from the other cars, and then turned off the engine.

Spike's mind spooled through the implications of a link between the dog man and Jake Cousins. How did they know each other? What did that mean in connection with the missing man? What were they up to in the flat?

It wasn't long before the communal door to the building opened and a figure came out. It was the dog man, Darren Rumsey, walking towards his van. It was the first time that Spike had seen him since the incident outside the court, and it brought back memories of the dash for safety from the pursuing hounds. Spike could still hear the snarling and the terrible scratching of claws on the road as they sought to gain traction while racing towards him. Perhaps they were in the van?

There was also the fact that the picture in the paper of him being attacked by the dogs may have had consequences for their owner, given that he had promised faithfully to keep them under control just a few minutes before he had turned them loose on him. All things considered, a face-to-face meeting with Mr Rumsey and his dogs was something that Spike needed to avoid.

Thankfully, Darren Rumsey didn't open the back. He walked straight to the driver's door and got in. Spike noted that he hadn't needed to unlock it. Maybe he knew that if someone had tried to steal it, they would have got a couple of his possessions that were a bit more of a handful than they had expected.

The van headed out of town, with Spike following at a discreet distance. The estate where Jake lived was already on the outskirts of the built-up area, but soon they were in open countryside, grass verges having replaced the kerbs of the developed part of town.

Spike tried to keep as far back as he could without losing sight of the van for more than a few seconds. He knew that if it turned suddenly into a side entrance while he was a long way behind, he could find himself cruising by without noticing and lose the van. But he also knew from what had happened with Susan Riley's husband that getting too close could be disastrous, maybe more so, for at least if he overshot he could retrace his steps. Discovery would blow his chances completely.

But the van didn't make any sudden turns. It continued along the same road as it became increasingly narrow, with thick hedges on either side, and the speed limit decreasing incrementally, until there was a road sign ahead. Spike slowed to a halt in front of it. It read: 'No through road. River ford.' The words gave Spike a feeling of unease.

Beneath them were more words, in a smaller type. They read: 'Unsuitable for light vehicles and all traffic in adverse weather conditions. Do not cross when in flood.' There was a picture in a red triangle with a wavy line over a road surface, indicating the water hazard.

A little way ahead the road provided a right turn, an alternative to heading for the river. Spike decided to take it, having seen a glimpse of the van carrying straight on. He drove past at first and then backed into it, continuing along in reverse for what he hoped was a safe distance, until he could just see the junction that he had come along through his windscreen, but not near enough to be visible to anyone driving past.

He switched off the engine and did what he always found himself doing in this sort of suspicious situation, began to compose a plausible explanation for his actions should he be asked to give one. It was a ploy that had worked well for him over the years. It was surprising how if you answered quickly and confidently, people were prepared to accept what you said as true. It was all in the delivery, he told himself.

There was an almost overwhelming silence here in the countryside. It had been quiet where he had parked outside the houses, but here it was so completely without any disturbance that Spike realised he was a long way from any form of habitation. When it got dark here, he thought, it would be completely black. There were no streetlights to guide you back to where you had come from. If you were walking here on a moonless night, it would be hard to see the road in front of your feet.

He realised that he didn't know exactly where he was. It reminded him of when he had followed a diversion once due to a road closure and ended up somewhere without having any idea of its location, as if a blindfold had been applied and he had been led there. It gave this place an eerie timelessness, as if he had been dropped in from the sky or had visited it from another lifetime. So much of what we do is linked to something – place, time, people – but this had none of these. All ties had been severed.

Spike was pulled out of his daydreaming by a flash of paintwork through the vegetation in front of him as a vehicle drove past the end of the road where he had come from. It gave him a fright for a moment, afraid that it might turn in to where he was, but it carried on past. He had been almost certain that it had been the van, but he waited for a few minutes before starting the engine and driving down to where the road divided. Turning left would lead back into town, the way that he had come and where the vehicle had just gone, and right would go towards the river. He steered his car to the right, knowing that he was driving down a no-through road.

After he had traveled along a few hundred yards of single-track lane, the hedges opened to reveal a small makeshift car park and beyond it the river. The road itself dipped and led directly into the water. The light grey of the concrete visible beneath the water right the way across the ford until it reached a short incline on the other bank. The flow was strong but steady, without the colour and turbulence of floodwater.

Spike turned into the car park, the loose stones crunching under his tyres. He was relieved to find it empty. Getting out, he walked to where the edge of the car park became the riverbank. A line of hand-sized stones had been arranged to separate the parking area from the grass, to deter drivers from venturing too close to the water's edge. He leaned against the trunk of a tall tree and peered into the margins but couldn't see the bottom, the current having scoured a deep hole close in.

A track led away from the car park, alongside the river, separated from it at intervals by trees. He followed the track for a few yards, not knowing what he was looking for, but feeling the need to explore and get an awareness of his surroundings.

A little way ahead there was a gap in the trees that made the water more visible, and when he reached it, he found a shingle beach that continued into the water, the main flow now having switched to the other side of the river. Spike stood in the opening, his face warmed by the sunshine, watching the water twist and turn past him, forming tiny whirlpools and eddies of surface bubbles as it hurried by beneath the low branches reaching across the surface and trailing in the water.

He remembered a phrase he had read, 'the ford at the River Bar', and he realised that this was it; this was where he was standing. The story he had read was about a female motorist who had tried to cross the river in her car, as she had done so many times before, but in the dark in winter. She had hesitated, seeing the rushing brown water, but had been late for an appointment and so had decided to take a risk.

It had been a couple of days later that the car had been found, having been lifted off the track by the force of the current and carried downstream, taking in water as it went.

Relatives had told the police her normal route, and divers had discovered her body in the car. There had been signs that she had tried desperately to open the door but been prevented by the weight of the water on the outside. Unable to break the glass, she had gradually run out of air as the level had risen inside, and then run out of life.

Spike gave an involuntary shudder as he thought how this was where it had happened, feeling cold for a moment as a cloud passed in front of the sun before it came out again. When you were a child, people would see you make that sudden spasm and say: 'Someone just walked over your grave.' It was funny how things came back to you from the distant past at moments such as this.

He walked a little further along the bank, but it all looked the same. There seemed no point in carrying on. He strolled back to his car in the otherwise empty car park, in this place that seemed to have been forgotten.

On the road back towards town he kept a close watch for any sign of the van, though now hoping that he wouldn't see it and risk being faced with a head-on confrontation, but it had gone. He drove past Jake Cousins' flat, but there was no sign of it, and then back past the dog man's house, but neither the van, nor the pensioner was around.

Outside his own home he sat in the car for a moment after switching off the engine, wondering what he had learnt, if anything. He tried to put himself in the mind of Jake and the dog man, what they were planning and how they would go about it. It had to be something to do with the river, but what, and when. One of Carl's quotations came to mind. Spike had been working in the office on a day of heavy rain and hadn't noticed quite how dark it had become, so engrossed had he been in his typing. Carl had come in with his customary flourish, swinging the door back as he made his entrance, and seen Spike bent over his keyboard struggling to read the words on the paper, having been too lazy to cross the room to flick the light switch on.

Carl had likened him to Bob Cratchit, bent over his work with only a candle to make it visible, only Carl had added a swear word in front of the Dickensian character's name. It made Spike smile as he recalled it. "'Let there be light!'" Carl had quoted as he had flicked the switch down. "'And there was light. And God saw that it was good.'" Then, warming to his theme as he took his coat off and drew back his chair, Carl had added: "What are you doing sitting here in the dark, you daft sod? 'The forces of evil seek out the darkness, that their deeds may be hidden from the eyes of the world, whereas the righteous man is drawn to the light.'"

Maybe that was it. If you were going to do something that you didn't want anyone to see, it had to be done after dark. But what would that mean for him, driving down narrow lanes with headlights giving away his presence, or with them switched off and not being able to see what was going on. He decided to go to bed early and get up while it was still night, to go back, first to the dog man's house, then to Jake's flat, and if the van wasn't outside either, down to the river.

It took Spike a while to fall asleep that night. It was still light outside, and made him think of his childhood days when bedtime had been while it was still daylight in summer and he would rather have been outside playing.

His thoughts began to stray, and when sleep came it was an anxious, disturbed slumber full of struggles to complete tasks that could never be finished. When he awoke, surrounded by darkness, the alarm brought a welcome end to the fretfulness of his dream, but then he remembered why he had set it, and a new heaviness weighed upon his mood.

He was fully awake now, washing and dressing quickly but not needing the splash of water on his face to focus his thoughts on the day ahead as he usually did. It was light enough not to need headlights, but only just, which is what he wanted.

He followed his plan, driving to the dog man's house, hoping to see the van, but aware at the same time that it was unlikely to be there. When it wasn't, he tried the flat, but with the same result. There was nothing for it but to make his way to the river.

The roads were quiet as he headed out of town, just a few workers on night shifts making their way home in their cars. The lightness of the traffic meant that birds lingered in the road ahead, reclaiming them for their territory while few people were around to drive them back into the hedgerows. At one spot a crow and a magpie quarreled over a roadkill in front of him, seeming not to notice Spike's car until it was almost upon them, then bursting into flight in different directions just yards from his front bumper as he slowed to a crawl.

Tentatively, Spike approached the lane with the sign for the ford, straining to see if a vehicle was visible in the car park. When he reached it, he found it empty, with a mixture of relief tinged with disappointment. He wanted something to happen, but not something that would endanger him, certainly not something that involved two angry dogs.

He parked where he had the previous day, switching off the engine and listening for the sound of any approaching vehicle, but the silence was as complete and unnatural as it had seemed when he had last been there. A thought that he had wasted his time and had got up early for nothing coloured his mood as he stood looking across the river, the sun beginning to show over the trees on the far side.

He looked around for any signs of activity since he had been there last, and noticed a tyre track in the mud where the road into the river parted from the entrance to the car park. He cursed himself for not noticing it the day before. Had it been there before? He couldn't tell.

As he walked towards the river where it passed the car park, he peered over the bank into the deep water, close in. A thought came to him that he was lower than he had been the day before, because he couldn't see over the tops of the grasses as well. At first, he couldn't understand how he could have shrunk overnight, but then he remembered how he had perched on top of the line of hand-sized stones to get a better view. He looked down at his feet, and where he was standing there were no stones, just a row of about a dozen or twenty hollows where they had been.

Spike stepped back rapidly to get a better look, running his eye along the row, which came to an end leaving a long gap before the line that it should have joined at a ninety-degree angle.

He looked around him, quickly, sure that someone must be watching, but there was nothing. His heart was beating hard now. He looked down at the stones again, and this time it was with a terrible sense of foreboding. Something had happened here in the few hours that he had been away. He had been right that this was the place that had been marked out in advance for something, and he had been right that whatever it was would happen in the dark. If he had come back in the night, whatever had happened could have involved him.

He took a deep breath. He needed to be logical. What would he do if he were the dog man? Where would he go? It would have been dark, so he wouldn't have gone far. Spike leaned over the bank to see if there was any sign of disturbance. The grasses were tangled, but that could have been the wind. Try further along, just past the next tree. And so, he made his way along the bank, walking downstream, stopping at intervals to look into the water and checking the vegetation for signs of it having been flattened.

He reached the beach, which was darker now without the sun on it, and the bough that stretched across the surface of the river. Small items of flotsam had gathered where the leaves trailed in the water, forming a small raft that obscured his view.

He went the other side of the track to the undergrowth and found an old branch of a tree that had snapped off, about an inch thick and five or six feet long. It was partially rotted and so weakened, but it could enable him to pull the raft towards him and see what was underneath.

It took several attempts to make it move, but once it began it came towards him, helped by the flow, which brought it towards his bank. There were a couple of small drink bottles on top of the layer of fallen leaves, and a discarded food carton.

130

With the debris in the edge, Spike used the branch to scrape away the top of the raft, and as he did so it rotated, turning beneath the water until something bobbed to the surface. Spike inched closer, trying to avoid shipping water into his shoes, and then he saw what it was.

He didn't react. He didn't believe what he was looking at, so how could he? He must be mistaken. He stared, still not fully comprehending, or not wanting to confirm what he had seen, but nothing changed. The hand floated to the surface, and stayed there.

Spike dropped the branch, which splashed loudly as it hit the water. He crouched down on his haunches on the small stones of the beach, and slowly, unstoppably, tears began to form in his eyes. At first, they were contained by his eyelashes, but as they grew, they started to run down his face and drip from his chin onto the ground between his feet. He pressed his finger and thumb into the corners of his eyes but that just made them sting, and the tears kept coming.

His nose was blocked and he had to sniff to breath, and then he heard a gasp, a sob even, and he realised he was crying, crying for the first time he could remember. Once he had started, he couldn't stop. His body was convulsed, gasping for air, the sound of his sobs loud, like a baby crying. He tried again to wipe away the tears, this time with the back of his hand, sniffing again to clear his nose, but he couldn't stop them.

He stumbled back along the track, almost falling as he misjudged the top of the bank, unable to see properly. The car seemed a long way away, but he made it there, gratefully, and sat inside, but the seclusion seemed to make his emotions well up even more and he broke down, his forehead on the steering wheel, his sleeve wet from the flood of tears on his face.

When eventually if ended, the sobs turned into coughing, and he leaned back in the seat, blinking, trying to drain his face and nose so that he could see and breath. It threatened to break out again, but he pushed the thoughts away with practical ones and felt the rush of emotion subside.

He started the car, unsure of whether it was safe to drive, but wanting to focus on something other than what he had just seen and felt. He knew where he was going. It was somewhere that he had always known that he would go eventually. The time hadn't been right before, but now he wanted to be there more than anywhere in the world.

It was far too early to be ringing the doorbell outside Sapphire's block of flats, but Spike did it anyway, not really caring what she would say. He waited, not knowing what he would do if she ignored the sound, but then he heard the buzz of the door being unlatched for him.

She was waiting at her door, probably having looked out of the window and seen his car. She was wearing a dressing gown, but looked as clear eyed and neatly groomed as she had when he had called before at more respectable hours.

Perhaps she could tell from the redness of his eyes that this wasn't the time for complaints about the early hour, or maybe the time of day indicated the seriousness of his visit, but there were no recriminations from her. "Come in," she said, almost as if she had been expecting him.

They sat in her living room, in the same seats that they had occupied before, Spike leaning forward so that his head almost reached his knees, but then sitting back trying to face her, knowing that he couldn't communicate with her with his face looking down.

"What's happened?" she asked, with that same soothing voice he had come to admire.

"You know what's happened," he told her, but in a resigned way.

"Yes, but you need to tell me."

"There was a body, in the river. I saw a hand, and I knew."

"When was this?" she asked, and the silence that followed confirmed that she had penetrated right to the core.

It took Spike a few moments before he could speak, the tears beginning again. "A long time ago. When I was just a boy. When we were both just boys."

"Who is we?"

"Me and my brother."

"Tell me what happened."

Spike swallowed, trying to compose himself. "We were down by the river, playing. He'd been making fun of me. And then he did it."

"Did what?"

"Dropped his guard. Just for a moment. He went to pick something up off the floor and he was there between me and the river, up above it on top of a wall. So I did it."

"Did what?"

"I pushed him. Not hard, but enough to make him lose his balance. He hung in the air for a second, his arms grabbing but with nothing to save him, falling backwards, looking at me, his face ugly with shock and fear. And I watched. I watched him fall and hit the water and then disappear."

"What did you do then?"

"I stood and watched, expecting him to come to the surface, but he didn't. For a long time I watched, not understanding. But I knew. I knew he couldn't swim. Then I ran to get help."

"And then?"

"They found him the next day. We were all there, looking. There was a shout, and I remember seeing a hand on the surface, white and lifeless. Then they pulled me away."

"What did you tell them?"

"I said it was an accident, that he had fallen. No one suspected. No one tried to blame me."

"But you blame yourself?"

"I know what happened. I know what I did, and that it can never be undone." Spike turned his head to face her, to see whether she was looking at him in a different way, but she was unchanged.

"You've carried this ever since, and now it's come back. But you can use the moment to move on, by forgiving yourself."

Spike couldn't see it. "I don't think I deserve forgiveness."

"Everyone deserves forgiveness. You're the only one who thinks it can't be yours."

Spike leaned right back, wiping his eyes, using a handkerchief to wipe his nose. He blinked to clear the wetness from his eyes and begin to gather himself to move forward.

"You are the only obstacle to starting again," she told him. "You are the one punishing yourself because you haven't been punished. But that has to end. Your suffering has to stop. You've paid for what you've done and must tell yourself that, to begin again."

"Yes," said Spike finally. "You're probably right."

"You know I'm right. You know that everything you've done since has been tainted by what happened, even your marriage, because you didn't feel you deserved good things to happen, but that's over now. You can stand alongside anyone else and not feel ashamed."

There was silence for a while as her words sank in. Spike even managed a watery smile. "How much do I owe you?" he asked.

"That's more like it," she said, smiling back. "I'll send you my bill."

As he got up to leave, they both heard a siren sounding on the street outside. They looked out of the window as a police car rushed by, but neither said anything. Only when Spike was downstairs again, beside his car, looking up at her standing at the window, and another car rushed by, followed by an ambulance, did he realise that what he had seen that morning had now been discovered.

Chapter 21

There was a young police officer standing in the road at the junction next to the sign for the ford, blocking Spike's path. Spike turned his car sideways on to the road down to the river and leant across to the passenger side of his car to wind down the window.

The officer bent down to speak to him. "I'm afraid you can't come through here. We've closed the road."

"Is there a problem?" asked Spike, feeling more composed now.

"There's an investigation taking place, so no one is allowed past this point."

"I'm a reporter with the *Bartown Chronicle*. Has something happened?"

The officer crouched down to be more on Spike's eye level and to get a better look at him, or perhaps just to rest his back. "You'll have to speak to our press officer to find out more. I'm not able to tell you anything."

Spike knew that he'd been told not to give anything away, not even a hint to a working journalist off the record. He turned his car around and headed back towards town, for once not bothered that he was excluded from the inner circle of those being provided with details, since he knew what they had found.

On his way back to the town he began to feel weary. A combination of the early morning and the shock of the day's events was beginning to make him feel drained. Everything seemed like a big effort. As he still had the rest of the day off, he decided to go home and catch up with some sleep, so that he would feel refreshed and able to decide what to do next.

The road home took him past the police station, and as he did so he saw a familiar vehicle parked in the car park at the front of the station. It was the grey van belonging to the dog man, and it made him jump in the same way that it had the day before, when he had been looking for it. This time, however, he could allow himself to relax and drive past while thinking what may be going on inside the building behind. Perhaps they had found something that linked him to the body and brought him in for questioning already.

At home he crawled into the bed he had left before first light that morning, still fully clothed, just needing to shut his eyes and forget for a while. He pushed his face under the top of the eiderdown to block out the daylight, feeling the warmth of his breath as it circulated around his face, lulling him to sleep.

It was over two hours later when he surfaced, at first unaware of his situation, but as he blinked the sleep from his eyes he remembered and sagged back into the pillow.

Getting up, he felt hungry, aware that he had skipped breakfast, so after tidying his hair and clothes he went out to the car and drove to a small parade of shops to get something to eat, the intention being to take it home and prepare a meal there.

As he came out of the small grocery store with a carrier bag of items, he looked along the road towards the newsagent's, preparing to unlock his car. A newspaper hoarding carried the headline for the first edition of the day's *Evening Post*. It read: 'Body found in River Bar'.

Spike opened the car door and swung the bag of food inside before striding towards the open door of the newsagent's. He bought a copy of the paper, not looking at it until he had got back to his car and was sitting inside.

He spread the front page of the broadsheet newspaper in front of him. The first words he read, under the headline, were: 'Exclusive report by Harry Dixon.'

The story said: 'The body of a man has been found in a river in a remote area of countryside on the outskirts of Bartown. Police divers were used to recover the remains this morning after attempts by officers to retrieve the body from the river had failed. The deceased, who is a white male believed to be in his sixties, was found to have been weighted down by putting large rocks in the pockets of his clothing, which meant that a specialist unit was needed to bring him to the shore. The grisly find was made by a dog walker exercising his two pets on the lane running alongside the river. The spot is the same one in which a woman's body was recovered from her car three years ago following heavy rain that made the ford impassable. A positive identification of the man has yet to be made, but police believe that a wallet and driving licence recovered from the scene suggest that it may be a local pensioner, Charles Appleby. Mr Appleby, who lived alone and had no close relatives, was recently served with a claim for compensation following a dispute over an accident in his garden involving his postman.'

Spike stopped reading. He couldn't take it in. He felt as if his face had been slapped, not once but twice, having already been bruised by seeing Harry Dixon's name alongside an 'exclusive' tag. First there was the news that the body had been found by a dog walker, and then the suggestion that it was Charles Appleby's. He looked back at the page, and there, close to the bottom, was a picture, Kat's picture, of the two men in the Horse & Barge, declaring a truce.

It felt as if the world had been knocked out of kilter. The man he had shared a drink with just days before was dead, and the missing man, Geoffrey Fellows, who he thought was gone, was still at large.

Maybe they had got it wrong. Maybe the driving licence and wallet had been planted. But to come out with the name in the story suggested near certainty.

There were quotes further down the story, from Chief Inspector James Parish, declaring that a murder investigation had been launched and that every effort would be made to catch the person or persons responsible. The road would be closed to traffic for some time, and he asked people to avoid the area.

A post mortem would be carried out to ascertain the cause of death, and an inquest opened when the findings were known. Anyone who had seen anything suspicious was asked to get in touch, and there would be an increased police presence in the town over the coming days to reassure the public.

Spike closed the paper and sagged back in his seat. Only the smell of the food wafting towards him reminded him that he was hungry. Still feeling in a daze, he drove home to gather his thoughts. As he passed a small florist's shop on the corner of a neighbouring street, he stopped outside and bought a bouquet of flowers, laying them in the foot well of the passenger side until he got home and could prop them in a dish of water.

As he ate, Spike turned things over in his mind. Some people liked to read at mealtimes, or listen to the radio or hold a conversation, but for Spike, the mere act of chewing seemed to make his thoughts develop and travel to places where they hadn't been.

He thought about Charles Appleby, and how moving a flowerpot seemed to have cost him his life, and Geoffrey Fellows, whose decision to leave his wife could yet cost him his. The common denominator seemed to be revenge. How pointless it seemed to an outsider, but he knew only too well that for those who succumbed to the temptation to get even, getting their own back felt like the most important thing in the world.

He finished his food and took the flowers to his car, heading for the Horse & Barge. He was pleased to find the pub fairly quiet, the lunchtime drinkers drifting away. He sat on a stool and waited for Sapphire to finish serving her customers before putting the bouquet on the bar. "It's by way of an apology, and a thank-you," he said, recalling how he had rung her doorbell while it was still getting light.

"You didn't need to do that," she said, putting them behind the bar, where there was a container of water, but he could see that she was pleasantly surprised.

"Maybe I can take you for a meal sometime, to make amends."

"How are you feeling?" she asked.

"Better than I was this morning. Different, I suppose. It feels different to have told someone, as if I've shared the burden."

"Good," she said. "That's an important step to make."

The landlord came through from the room behind the bar and tossed the latest edition of the *Evening Post* on the top for customers to read. Spike reached over and laid the front page out on the surface. The story was the same as in the first edition, but another picture had been added. It was of a man on crutches being led across the police station car park. The caption read: 'Local postman Reggie Patterson is being questioned by police in connection with the discovery of the body.'

As he was reading, Spike could see Sapphire watching him, taking in his expression as he looked at the story. He knew she was wondering whether he still wished that it had been his name on the byline instead of Harry Dixon's. There was a phone number given for anyone to ring with information, which Spike jotted down in his notebook.

136

Sapphire glanced at the story. "So, your missing man is still missing. You're right back where you started."

Spike only half heard her, still scanning the newspaper, but as her words slowly penetrated his thoughts and registered with him, he looked up suddenly with a jerk of his head, staring ahead of him unseeingly. "Say that again," he said, slowly, turning towards her.

"You're right back where you started," she repeated.

"Back where I started," he looked away again, into empty space. "Yes. That's where I should be. I should be right back where I started."

He folded the paper and put it back on the bar. "I've just realised I need to be somewhere. I'll be in touch when I've got it sorted. Sorry," he said, hurrying out of the pub to his car.

It seemed to take a long time to reach his destination, though he knew the way well. He passed the house where he had interviewed Isabelle Fellows about her missing husband, but he didn't stop, not until he was a little way short of the lay-by in the country lane leading away from town.

As he'd done once before, he backed his car off the road and into the entrance to a field, where it was hidden behind the thick hedgerows, and turned off the engine, allowing enough room to see the entrance to the wood a little further along on the opposite side of the road.

He was glad that he'd had something to eat. He knew he could be there for some time, and he didn't want to listen to his stomach rumbling as it demanded to be fed, knowing that he couldn't leave. But everyone needs to eat at some stage, and that was why he was here.

It was a gamble, he knew, a guess, but if the missing man had to be hidden in a hurry, and the police were asking everyone to keep a watch out for anything suspicious following the body in the river, it was a place that could be considered unlikely to attract attention.

He wondered what Geoffrey Fellows was thinking now, with all this time to reflect on his actions and consider his future. Of course, it could already be too late, he may have gone the same way as Charles Appleby, but if someone has no connection with their victim, a hired killer with no anger towards the person in their sights, and with their own safety from discovery uppermost in their mind, maybe, just maybe, they would hold back until the state of high alert had eased.

Spike slid his hand in his pocket and found the key to the hut. He also had the silver half-heart ornamental fob that Susan had made, inscribed with the word 'Hers'. He turned it over in his hand, like a lucky charm, hoping that holding it would give him the break that he so badly needed.

His thoughts began to wander. Occasionally a car would come by, but none of them stopped. He shifted uncomfortably in the driver's seat, wondering whether you could get bedsores from sitting too long in the front seat of a car. He tried to stretch out his legs, to ease the stiffness in his muscles, but the pedals prevented him getting the desired relief.

He yawned and glanced at his watch. Other people had fun on their days off, he thought. How many would spend them sitting in a car on a track next to a quiet road watching the birds flit past while they got on with their busy lives?

At least he'd had plenty of sleep, so there was no danger of him nodding off. He'd just thought that when he heard another vehicle engine coming along the road, but this one sounded slightly quieter, as if it wasn't traveling at the usual speed. It could be wishful thinking, of course, but he allowed himself to hope.

As it came by, he glanced up at the windscreen but with his head still down, not wanting to show his face to the driver in case they were looking his way, and his heart gave a leap. He knew what it was straight away. He had seen so much of it in the past two days. There was no mistaking the dog man's grey van.

It slowed still further, as he knew now it would, and pulled into the lay-by further up the road on the other side. The dog man got out and looked around. Spike was afraid he would be seen, but the man was in a hurry, and a quick glance up and down the road for any traffic coming his way was all that he needed.

In his hand was a small paper bag, and Spike recognised the distinctive striped blue-and-white pattern as belonging to the bakery in town that he knew so well. The dog man strode into the wood, still glancing around him, and disappeared.

Spike's heart was pounding, not just from the fear of discovery but also the thought that he could finally be on the brink of success. He wanted to punch the air, but he knew that would be premature, as well as inadvisable. So he waited some more, only this time knowing that the odds had swung in his favour.

It wasn't long before the dog man reappeared, and this time he was trotting, such was his haste to get back to his van. He had something in his hand, something black and knitted, like a wooly hat, which he was stuffing into his pocket but failing each time because his coat was bouncing as he jogged along.

Glancing up the road for one last time, he jumped inside and drove away, leaving just a light trail of exhaust fumes dispersing gently in the still air.

When the sound of the van's engine had faded, Spike started his car and headed back towards town, in the opposite direction. What he was going to do next was a gamble, but having guessed and won already, he felt confident that it would lead where he wanted.

Outside the small terraced house, he knocked on the familiar front door and saw it opened by the welcoming figure of Kat's mother. She invited him in, but he said he was in a bit of a hurry, so she called her daughter from upstairs.

"I've got a job for you, if you're free," he told her, and organised as usually she had her kit ready to go. Soon they were in the car, driving back to the lay-by and the same track opposite, where he could back out of sight, but only after he had stopped at the last public phone box before his destination.

Spike had rested his notebook on the ledge next to the phone and dialed the number that he had copied from the paper. When a man's voice had answered, he had told him that there seemed to be some activity at the entrance to the wood where the retired teacher had gone missing, as if something suspicious were going on there. When he had been asked for his name, he had said he didn't want to give it, and hung up.

It was less than a mile to the track opposite the lay-by, and he had got parked back in position by the time three police cars came speeding up to the entrance to the wood, the officers inside running in to investigate. It was several minutes later when they emerged, this time at a very much slower pace, helping a grey-haired man who looked unsteady on his feet to walk, a length of chain attached to one of his ankles trailing behind him.

Kat was ready with her camera, taking discreet photographs from beside the hedge with her long lens.

Two of the police cars turned and drove back the way they had come, the officers in the third one going back into the wood, looking around on the ground and in the bushes as they went. When they were out of sight, Spike started the car, and he and Kat made their way to her home.

She recognised the man being led away as the same one that she had photographed in Susan Riley's back garden. "If what you say is true," she suggested, "he's lucky to be alive."

"There's that saying that revenge is a dish best served cold," said Spike. "But when it goes too cold, no one has the appetite to eat it. Geoffrey Fellows could have been killed when he was found in the back garden, but the longer it was put off, the greater the chance that he would live." He realised he'd used a quotation to strengthen his argument. "I'm starting to sound like Carl," he said. "Maybe I've been spending too much time in his company."

"Talking of spending time with someone, I've been offered a job with the *Evening Post*. They've been giving me a bit of freelance work. I did the picture of the postman on crutches at the police station for Harry Dixon. They like what I've done and say there's a permanent post if I want it."

Spike was sad to hear it. It was good to have a colleague that he could rely on and who was easy to work with. "That would be a shame."

"I'd still be covering this area," she said, sensing his disappointment, "but I'd be working for them rather than being available for hire." They reached the front of her mother's house. "I haven't said yes. I said I'd think about it."

"You should do it," said Spike, trying to sound pleased for her. "It's a big opportunity."

"Yes," she said, rather dolefully. "Anyway, I'll get these pictures done and get them through to you." Spike watched her go inside, and then turned his car towards home, his sense of elation now tempered with feelings of regret.

Chapter 22

It seemed like more than two days since Spike had last climbed the worn steps leading to the office. So much had happened, it felt more like a fortnight. Tom was in the back, the fragrant smell of pipe smoke wafting into the reporters' room. Spike shed his jacket onto his chair and walked through to speak to him.

His boss looked up from his work. "Hello. Had a good couple of days?"

Spike deflected the question with one of his own. "Anything happened while I've been away?"

Tom tossed a folded copy of the *Evening Post* across the desk towards him, the front-page story visible.

"Yes, I saw that," said Spike.

"Your friend the flowerpot man. Can you put together a rehash of the story for us from what they've said and find a new angle to re-nose it slightly? I still want to lead with it, even though everyone knows about it."

"You could just go with a story about how the missing man has been found. I've got pictures of it happening and of him when he was in hiding."

Tom took his pipe out of his mouth and rested it on the ashtray on his desk, perhaps fearing that it might fall out of his mouth as his jaw dropped open. "When did that happen?"

"Last night. He'd been kidnapped and taken to the hut. He'd been hiding in the home of a family friend who'd just split up with her husband. They were planning a new life together, but her husband found out and paid a friend who fancied himself as an amateur hit man to bump him off, only he'd already been approached by his postman to get rid of the flowerpot man."

Tom tapped his pipe out on the ashtray. "Can you prove any of that?"

Spike had known that proving what he knew would be the difficult part. He recalled from his training days many years before that knowing something was no defence against libel actions if you couldn't prove it was true. Without proof, you were easy pickings. It was what prompted the saying among hacks that only half of what they found out ever made it into print.

"So, what can you say definitely?" asked Tom, practical as ever, having a paper to bring out.

"Well, I could go back to the house where they're living and try to get an interview with the missing man and his new partner. The *Evening Post* will no doubt have the story about him being found, but they won't have the picture and probably won't have an interview with him yet. I could have the advantage, because I've talked to her before. The story about the body in the river can be used alongside it on the front page, but you'll have the new angle that you want, and maybe even hint at a link between the two."

Spike could tell that Tom liked the idea, and he was soon putting his jacket back on and heading for the door. It had sounded good while he had been saying it, but he knew that getting the couple to agree to talk about what had happened would be another matter. But he had found in life that it was better to impress people by telling them what you could deliver first, and then worry about how you were going to manage it afterwards, rather than leave them feeling underwhelmed by a wishy-washy pitch.

As he drove along the road where Susan Riley lived, Spike half expected to find her husband sitting in a car on the other side of the road outside her house, as he had been last time he'd been there, but common sense told him that he would be keeping out of the way for now.

Everything seemed to be in place again since his last visit. The blue Peugeot car was back in the drive, and the doormat that had been kicked to one side was back where it belonged.

Spike tapped on the knocker and waited for a response. It was Susan who answered the door, looking agitated but then slightly relieved that it was only the man from the newspaper and not something more problematic.

"I understand it's good news about Geoffrey. He's been found." Spike reasoned that appearing to be ignorant of her part in hiding him would work in his favour. The less she knew about his close monitoring of the case, the better in terms of winning her over.

"Yes. I'm very relieved," she said.

"Is he okay after what happened?"

"He seems to be," she said, and then pursed her lips, as if she wished she hadn't.

"You've had a chance to meet him?" he asked, as if surprised that a family friend would already have access.

"Ah, yes." She thought for a moment. "Actually, he's here with me now."

Spike fought back a smile. "Really? Would it be possible to talk to you both, to give people an idea of what he's been through?" Spike could see her thawing. In her mind she was weighing up whether to try to hide or whether explaining it all would be the first step to taking the attention away from them and making it all go away as people moved on.

"Maybe that would be best," she said. "I had another man from a newspaper at the door earlier, wanting to talk, one I didn't know. I turned him away, but I thought afterwards that I can't keep doing that, jumping whenever I hear a knock at the door." She stepped aside. "You'd better come in."

She led the way into her living room, and there, seated at first but getting up as Spike entered, was the missing man. It felt like being in the presence of a celebrity, and Spike wanted to say to him: 'We meet at last,' but knew he shouldn't. He had to choose his words carefully and make it appear that he knew nothing about what had been going on.

The three of them sat in a triangle on the three-piece suite, and Geoffrey Fellows, retired teacher turned author, told him what had happened.

"Susan and I have been friends for a while, and my marriage was over. We used to meet for a few hours each day, and then she and her husband split up, so I came here. Each time we met, I didn't want to go back at the end of the day, so one day I just decided I wouldn't. It seemed like the right thing to do. No more pretending I was going to the writing hut, no more saying the work had been slow. I didn't have to make excuses anymore."

"So you hid here?" asked Spike.

"Yes, but it wasn't that difficult. No one came looking, and if someone came to the door I would just go out into the back garden."

"But you knew that the police were trying to find you?"

"I was aware that they were looking, which is why I hid one of my old shoes from the hut in the wood beside the lay-by, but I thought in time they would give up and go away. I didn't want to face all the problems and upset to everyone of ending my previous life, so I walked away from it. It just seemed like the best way."

"But what if Susan's husband had found out?" Spike suggested.

"That seems to have been what happened. I was in the back garden. Susan had gone to the shops. I was on a lounger in the sun, reading a book, and suddenly something was pulled over my head, some sort of hat that acted as a blindfold, and I was pulled along, not being able to see where I was going, and through the house into a car and driven away. My hands were tied behind my back, so I couldn't take the blindfold off, and when it was, I found that I was in my hut.

"There was a man there, tall with strong arms covered in tattoos. I couldn't see his face because he was wearing a balaclava. He untied my hands, but only after he had put a dog chain around my ankle and attached the other end to a metal hoop that he'd hammered into the floor.

"He brought me food a couple of times, and then the police arrived and managed to get me free."

"What do you think would have happened to you?" asked Spike.

"I don't know. I don't like to think about it."

"Do you think you're lucky to be alive?"

"I think you could say that, yes. The police insisted I went to the hospital last night for a check-up, but they said I have no obvious injuries and should just rest to get over the shock."

"Did the police want to know why you didn't come forward when they were looking for you?"

"There was a mention of it, but I think they probably felt that now wasn't the time for a telling off, and that they were just glad to find me still in one piece. I think they will be back for a statement at some stage down the line, but I think they have got their hands full with enquiries about that body that was found in the river."

"What about Susan's husband?"

Geoffrey looked at Susan. "We've decided to sell the house and the wood and move away. Start again somewhere new."

Susan added: "We just want to put all this behind us and get back to leading a normal life."

"What about your wife?" Spike asked Geoffrey.

The man picked at his fingers, nervously. "I will have to face her, yes, but moving away should make it easier."

As Spike thanked them both and got up to leave, he asked one final question, as an afterthought.

"One thing I was going to mention. Does the name Jake Cousins mean anything to you?"

Geoffrey Fellows looked surprised. "If you mean Jacob Cousins, I taught him back in my days at the college."

"What was he like?"

"I think 'difficult' would be the kindest word for him. He seemed to take against me. Decided that I had ruined his chances of following his chosen career."

"You didn't, then?"

"He did a much better job of that than I could ever have done. His work was always poor, but it was easier to blame others, me in particular, than to work harder at getting better grades." He paused for a moment. "You don't think that he had anything to do with all this, do you? That was a long time ago."

"I don't know for sure," Spike told him. "But since you plan to move away, maybe it won't matter."

He said goodbye to the couple on their doorstep and was soon in his car driving back towards the office. All he needed to do now was keep what he had obtained away from Harry Dixon until the paper came out, which was why he decided to write the story at home, bringing it into the office typed out ready for Tom. After that, it was out of his hands.

But before he did so he had one last visit to make. He hoped that Isabelle Fellows would be at home, and although she wasn't gardening at the front, as on his previous visit, she answered the door when he rang the bell.

She invited him in, a look of weary resignation on her face. "No doubt you've heard?" she said.

Spike felt sorry for her. Her husband had been found, safe and well, but it wasn't the outcome that she had wanted. "How are you coping?" he asked.

"Still taking it in, I suppose," she said. "Just feeling... empty."

Spike noticed that the framed photo of her with her husband and Susan on holiday together, which he had borrowed and returned, had been put away.

"You didn't suspect, when he vanished?"

"Anything was possible. There were so many possible outcomes. I just wanted to know what had happened."

"And now that you do?"

"I don't know that knowing is any better. In a way it's worse." She looked away for a moment. "And everyone will know now, that he left me. They'll know that he would rather have been missing than be married to me." She turned her face back towards Spike. "Is it better to lose someone you love than to lose their love while they're still alive?"

Spike didn't answer. Instead, he put his hand in his pocket and took out the silver key fob that belonged to her. He held it out. "I told you I'd find him, and you told me to give you back the keyring when I did."

"Yes, I remember," she said. "That seems like a long time ago. Some promises are kept, but others get broken." She looked at the fob, still in Spike's outstretched hand. "You keep it," she said. "Maybe it will bring you more luck than it did me."

Tom had filled Carl in about the missing man discovery when Spike eventually returned to the office, so when Spike came through the door of the reporters' room, he was greeted with: "Aha. The missing man returneth."

There were times when Carl's banter wearied Spike, but this was one occasion when it made him smile. Having succeeded in what he had wanted to do, he was willing to listen to the good-natured ribbing, content in the knowledge that it was job done.

"I can see the headlines now," continued Carl. "'Missing man cheats death in love nest snatch. Former teacher's love lessons end in detention.'"

"Maybe I could throw one of your quotations back at you," countered Spike. "'Oh ye of little faith, wherefore didst thou doubt?'"

"Fair play to you," admitted Carl. "You did find him, and still alive as well, unlike your flowerpot man, who's now pushing up daisies himself."

Being detached from the people involved in the stories enabled Carl to be flippant about events seen only from a distance. Spike knew that it would be different if he had met any of them in person.

"What I want to know," Carl insisted, "is how did you know where to find him? Who told you he was there?"

Now it was Spike's turn to make fun. "Haven't you heard? A journalist never reveals his sources."

"Was it your death threat man, turning in his accomplice to save his own skin?"

"That's the only thing I'm not sure about in this whole affair," said Spike, being more serious. "Whether Jake Cousins was involved, but was told that there was already a contract out to get rid of the missing man, so he didn't need to carry out his threat and could just watch from the sidelines."

One of the ladies from the front office came in with copies of the first edition of the *Evening Post*. She handed one each to Carl and Spike and then took one through to Tom before going back out.

Spike glanced at the front cover and, even with it folded in half, he could tell that Harry Dixon had supplied the front-page lead story again. He had the missing man news, though without a picture, but he also had 'Murder case prime suspect freed', with a picture of the postman on crutches.

It read: 'The prime suspect in the body-in-the-river murder hunt has been released by police after lengthy questioning revealed insufficient evidence to bring charges. Postman Reggie Patterson was told he was free to go after no link was found between him and the discovery of the body of pensioner Charles Appleby, whose remains were found in the River Bar close to the ford.

'Mr Patterson told the *Evening Post* in a statement prepared with his solicitor: "I'm pleased to have been able to clear my name in connection with the investigation into the death of Charles Appleby and to show that I had no involvement in what happened to him. Ever since the discovery of his body, fingers have been pointing at me because of our falling out. But I would like to remind people that we settled our differences before the unfortunate events that led to his death and so I am in no way a part of what happened. The mere fact that I have been unable to walk without crutches for some time, due to my having a heavy plaster cast on my leg, should have made it obvious to everyone that I could not have committed the crime. Having now proved my innocence and been exonerated of all blame, I would like to resume my life without any shadow hanging over me in connection with this case."

'A spokesman for the police said: "Although Mr Patterson has been released without charge, investigations are still ongoing and if further evidence comes to light that incriminates any specific parties in the case, these will be investigated fully and those involved held to account."'

Spike and Carl finished reading the story and looked at each other. "So Postman Patterson reckons he's got away with it," said Carl. "I hope he paid the bloke who did it enough to keep him silent. He'll be twitching now until he knows they've dropped the case. That's the trouble when you get up to mischief – you never know when it's going to come back and bite you on the bum."

Tom wandered through from his office, and Spike gave him the story that he had written of the missing man interview. "How did it go?" he asked.

"Better than I expected. I'd thought he might be tight-lipped, but he seemed glad to finally explain what had happened, as if it lightened the load. It sounds as if Harry Dixon got to them before me but was rebuffed, which is handy. So much for his claim that if you want to get an interview with someone, you have to pretend to be their friend."

"You still think the two stories are linked?"

"I'd put money on it. But there's only one man who knows for sure, and he's going to be keeping quiet, especially if he's now been paid to carry out two killings but only managed one. No wonder the missing man is leaving town."

Tom went back into his office to read Spike's words, commenting as he went: "Maybe you should take days off more often. Everything seems to happen while you're away."

Carl had been leafing through the rest of the paper while they had been talking, and suggested to Spike that he might like to take a look at page ten. Spike found the page in his copy of the paper and saw a photo of two men in black bow tie evening dress, one presenting the other with an award. The headline read: 'Reporter scoops Journalist of the Year'. The story beneath it said: 'Our man Harry Dixon was named Journalist of the Year at the annual press awards for his regular exclusive stories for the *Evening Post*. The talented newsman beat off stiff competition from an impressive line-up of shortlisted candidates to clinch the title, which was presented to him by Chief Inspector James Parish of the local police force at a gala evening at the local theatre. Harry has also recently branched out into lecturing on journalism, having received bookings from schools and colleges wishing to tutor their pupils and students in their career choices and the benefits to society of responsible reporting.'

Spike looked across at Carl as he closed the newspaper and folded it. "I thought you'd like that one," grinned Carl.

Spike didn't reply, he just dropped his copy of the paper in the bin.

When he got home that evening, Spike could see that the Barratts were back from their holiday. Their estate car was in the drive, he could hear the sound of young feet running up and down the stairs, and Mrs Barratt had been around with her vacuum and carried out her customary spring-cleaning spree. She liked opening the French windows that linked Spike's room with the front garden, along with the back door and the one that led from his room to his kitchen. A strong breeze was blowing right through his part of the house, sending sheets of paper from the table at the end of his bed to the downwind side of the room, where they fluttered against the skirting boards. It was at times such as this that he wondered if he should find somewhere else to live, but this was cheap and mostly hassle free, so he just rode out the bumps along the way.

The Tupperware dish that Spike had washed and dried had been reclaimed and replaced with a note apologising for not remembering to say in her previous note what the contents had been. She informed him that the pink goo had been strawberry blancmange, which made Spike glad that he hadn't tried to warm it up in the microwave before eating it.

There was also a letter for him, and Spike could tell from the handwriting that it was from his mother. He leaned back against the kitchen's work surface as he opened it, watched by the family's feline friend, Slug, the cat no doubt wondering whether there was food inside.

His mother often wrote to him when she was arranging something that he might like to attend, preferring to put pen to paper than ring him at the office, since he had no access to a phone at home. She wanted him to know that there was an anniversary coming up, the thirtieth since the death of his brother. She and his father would be going back to the spot where he had been found, beside the river, to mark the occasion, and she was asking him whether he would like to be there, too. He folded the letter and put it back in the envelope. It was a journey that he had made many times with his parents over the years. Maybe this time it would feel different.

146

Chapter 23

The inquest into the death of Charles Appleby was held at the town's magistrates' court, though the coroner was from outside the area. Robin Baker-Soames had the task of weighing up the evidence and reaching a verdict on how the pensioner had met his end.

Spike was in his familiar position at one of the tables allocated to the press when the court usher ordered all to rise for the arrival of the barrister who would be conducting the proceedings.

He began by calling for evidence to be produced to indicate that the deceased was the man in question, which was provided by a police officer, and he then questioned the officer about whether the death was likely to result in criminal charges being brought, which would mean adjourning the hearing until the court case had been heard.

Sergeant Bryan Collins told him that no charges had been brought in connection with the case, and that there were no immediate plans to charge anyone with causing the death of the deceased until further evidence came to light. He said that one person had been questioned at length but had been released without charge. He said that evidence had been collected showing fresh tyre tracks at the scene, but that they had matched the vehicle being driven by the dog walker who had found the body.

In light of this information, the coroner indicated that the inquest could go ahead, and called on a local pathologist, Dr Alan Pryce, to give evidence to suggest how, where, why and when the victim had died. Dr Pryce told the court that his post-mortem showed trauma to the right side of head of the deceased, causing bruising to the right temple consistent with a blow to that area. However, he added that this injury might have been caused by him falling when entering the river.

An examination of the lungs showed their weight to be heavier than normal and, as such, consistent with drowning, but the lack of air bubbles suggested that there was no desperate attempt to breath while in the water.

"Whether this was because he was already dead, or whether he was unconscious in the water from the blow to the head and died when water subsequently entered his lungs, is not possible to ascertain," he said.

"The stones in the pockets of the deceased's clothing may have been placed there by a person or persons responsible for his death, but equally they could have been put there by the deceased himself to weight his body prior to entering the river.

"Although no vehicle was found at the scene, it is possible that the deceased could have made his way there on foot. It is therefore not possible to conclude one way or the other whether Mr Appleby died at his own hands or those of another, nor whether he died in the water or a short time before entering it."

As he was listening to the evidence, Spike was distracted by a cough up in the public gallery of the court. Looking up for a moment as the next witness settled himself prior to giving evidence, Spike saw a familiar face among the few observers watching the proceedings, that of Jake Cousins.

Charles Appleby's neighbour was called to give evidence, and he told the inquest that he had seen the deceased in his garden the day before the discovery of his body and that he had seemed in good spirits.

He explained that he had heard nothing untoward in the vicinity of his neighbour's house during that evening or the night, though he said that his bedroom was on the opposite site of his house from that of his neighbour's property.

"I noticed the next morning that his living room curtains had not been drawn back when I went out for a paper," he recalled. "I knew he was an early riser, so I rang the doorbell, but got no response, which is when I called the police."

Having heard the evidence presented to him, Robin Baker-Soames declared that an open verdict would be recorded, and that the body could be released for burial or cremation.

He also noted that the deceased had no next of kin, being unmarried and living alone with no surviving siblings, though he added: "As I understand it there are sufficient funds in his estate to meet the cost of a funeral."

Kat had been booked to take photos of the witnesses and the coroner as they left the inquest, and Spike was able to point out which were the ones whose evidence would be used in his report. She stood well back beside the entrance to the car park with a long lens, taking photos as individuals broke away from the groups that knew each other and descended the steps that led away from the terrace in front of the doors to the court. As she turned away from the building towards where Spike had parked his car, she saw one of the people he had asked her to photograph leaning over the front of Spike's car's windscreen.

Instinctively she reached for a second camera with a shorter lens that was hanging from her shoulder to fire off a shot. The man was walking away, but as she looked through the lens he turned, perhaps to check that the object he had left under the car's wiper blade was still in place. As he did so, she pressed the shutter release, capturing him looking back towards what was in the foreground pinned to the windscreen.

Spike had been watching the people involved in the court case leave, but he turned on hearing the sound of Kat's camera firing, to see what she had been photographing. His eye followed the direction of her lens, to see Jake Cousins walking away along the street. He thought for a moment that she had wanted to get another picture of him from behind, but then he could see what looked like an envelope flapping under his car wiper blade.

Together they walked towards the car, Jake now well along the street. Spike lifted the wiper and picked up the envelope. He opened it and peered inside, and then gave Kat a knowing look.

"What's in there?" she asked, her curiosity piqued.

"Get in the car and I'll show you," said Spike, and they took their seats in the front.

"Put out your hand," he said to her, and when she did he tipped the object onto her palm. It was a silver key fob. She turned it over and read the inscription, the word 'His' printed in italics.

"Why has he left you a key fob?" she asked.

Spike didn't answer. Instead, he dipped his hand in his pocket and pulled out another one, almost identical but the mirror image of the one that she held. He put it in her hand alongside the first and she read the inscription 'Hers'.

Kat could see what it was now, and she drew the two halves together to form a heart, the first time the two sides had been united since the missing man saga had begun. "Is this something that the woman who made the jewellery did?" She handed the halves back to Spike, who fitted the two sides together again to look at them.

"Yes. She made it for Geoffrey Fellows and his wife." He looked at it in the palm of his hand for a moment. "I wonder whether Susan knew when she was making it for them that it would be she who would break them apart."

Kat had her car with her, because she had made her own way to the court while the inquest had been taking place. She put her cameras and lenses in her case and made as if to leave. "By the way," she said. "I've accepted the job on the *Evening Post*."

"I'm glad," he said. "You'll enjoy it. You're a talented photographer. Not much gets past you."

"It's half anticipation and half luck," she said, modestly. "I enjoy the challenge."

"As Gary Player is supposed to have said: 'The harder I practise, the luckier I get.'"

"Now you really are starting to sound like Carl."

As she opened the car door to leave, she leaned across and gave Spike a kiss on the cheek. She turned back towards him, pausing before closing the door. "Just saying goodbye," she said.

Spike had been planning to go back to the office after the inquest, but he found himself making a detour just because it felt right. He bounced the wheels of his car up the high kerb and parked on the front drive, still not quite sure why he was there, but just wanting to be.

As he went to press the button for Sapphire's flat, a woman came out through the entrance and noticed him there. She saw him press the button as she was closing the door and said: "She's not here." Spike looked towards her. "She's gone away. The woman who lived in that flat, if that's who you wanted. She's moved out. The landlord needed it for someone else, so she had to leave."

Spike stepped back and glanced up at the window, but it was empty. "Did she say where she was going?"

"No. It was all a bit of a rush. I didn't know her that well." She looked along the street and then back at Spike. "Sorry," she said. "I'd better go."

Spike got back into his car and drove away. When he reached the Horse & Barge, he pulled into the car park and made his way inside. He looked through the gloom of the interior towards the bar, thinking he might see her there, but the landlord was serving drinks to his customers.

When he was free, Spike asked if Sapphire was coming in at lunchtime. "She's handed her notice in," he told Spike, looking at him slightly suspiciously. "Said she needed to leave."

Spike thanked him and made his way back outside. He paused for a moment, unsure of which way to turn, and then instead of going to his car, he walked along the high street until he reached a small church, set back from the other buildings. He walked up the short path and tried the big metal handle of the heavy wooden door, which clicked and opened for him.

Inside was even darker than in the pub, with a musty smell of hymn books and furniture polish, but as his eyes became accustomed, he could see the rows of pews leading to an ornate altar, up a set of steps at the other end of the church, lit by sunlight shining through a stained-glass window.

There was complete silence inside. Even the traffic on the busy street outside didn't disturb the sense of calm, filtered out by the thick stone walls. Spike knelt in one of the pews and looked up at the altar. He stayed like that for several minutes, his jumble of thoughts gradually unraveling. Leaning there, his forearms resting on the wood, his hands together, he asked for forgiveness for what he'd done and what he hadn't done.

When he felt at peace, he made his way back the way he had come in, but paused beside a small table on which there was a stack of service sheets used by the congregation. He took the two key fobs out of his pocket and laid them down on the table, the silver surface of the jewellery making two audible clicks as he put them down together, before going back outside, glad to be leaving them behind.

A few days later, Spike was in the office when the first editions of the *Evening Post* were brought through. The front page had a story headlined: 'Bodies of two men found in house'. Below the headline it read: 'Neighbours raised alarm after violent row'. 'Two dogs taken from house in cages'.

The story, an exclusive by Harry Dixon, explained: 'The bodies of two men have been recovered from a house on an estate in Bartown after neighbours heard a "blazing row" and called police. One man in his fifties died from multiple stab wounds, while the other man, in his forties, appears to have been mauled to death by two dogs. It took a team of specialist officers armed with bait and reinforced steel cages several minutes to subdue the animals, which prevented ambulance staff from accessing the house to provide emergency medical treatment. A large kitchen knife was recovered from the scene.'

There was a photo of specialist unit police officers in protective clothing carrying the two cages containing the dogs out of the house. Beneath the photo was the line: '*Evening Post* photographer Kat Bishop captured the moment when the dogs were removed.'

The story continued: 'Neighbours reported hearing male voices raised in an argument that included references to money, followed by screams. A pensioner living across the road rang the police, but those attending needed to send for officers trained in dealing with dangerous dogs before they could enter the property.

'A large amount of cash was recovered from a carrier bag in a wardrobe in the bedroom belonging to the property's tenant, some of which police believe may have been a payment in connection with a crime carried out on behalf of another person.

'Local resident Ralph Pearson said: "It sounded like two blokes having a blazing row to me, and then all hell broke loose, with screams and dogs barking and growling and more screaming. People were coming out of their homes, but none of us dared go in to help, not with them dogs in there."

'Chief Inspector James Parish said: "Officers responding to reports of a disturbance yesterday evening managed to contain the threat posed by what we believe to be two Japanese fighting dogs, the owner of which was known to police.

"Unfortunately, by the time that it was safe to attend to the occupants of the house, it was too late to save them, despite the best efforts of the medical emergency team.

"The scene that greeted my officers when they were able to get inside the house was a distressing one, for both them and for those whose job it is to gather evidence after such events.

"However, while further investigations will take place into what has happened at the house, I would like to reassure the public that we are not looking for anyone else in connection with what has occurred."'

The following weekend, Spike was in the back of his parents' car on their way to the river not far from their home. It reminded him of journeys made in the days of his youth, before learning to drive had liberated him from that familiar view, watching the world over the backs of their heads and through the side window. His brother had been beside him back then. What would he have been like now?

He thought about anniversaries and how popular they were with the news media, for no reason other than the matrix of a calendar. Old wounds partially healed were opened and laid bare, old grievances reignited and the glowing embers of indignation fanned into flames once more, and for what, a random date in time. But it was customary to remember when that anniversary came around once more.

The riverbank looked the same as it had always done at this time of year. It seemed to Spike as if every riverbank was the same, the trees pushing their roots into the water, that same damp odour and the low vegetation scattered with the decaying remains of last autumn's leaves. It could be any river in England, and every river now made him feel sad.

He had wondered whether it would feel different this time, now that he had shared his secret. There were new voices in his head this time, Chief Inspector Jim Parish asking him if he was a cold-hearted killer, and Sapphire telling him to forgive himself, along with Carl saying: 'Am I my brother's keeper?'. He could hear them as he walked along the path to the spot where the body had been found.

One thing that remained the same was the sense of expectation that something would happen when they got there, a sense of anticipation, as if there would be something there to observe, but knowing all along that there would be nothing, like going to a football match or a concert only for it to be cancelled, and coming away feeling unfulfilled.

This time, however, his father had a bag over his shoulder, from which he took a small camera. He asked a passing dog walker, a lady with a black Labrador, to take a photo of the three of them, their backs to the river, which she did, looking slightly awkward as she did so, happiest when she could hand the camera back again, not calm and confident like Kat would have been. Maybe she might even have made them smile.

Spike knew that one day he would find that photo tucked inside an album in a cupboard, slightly yellowed with age, a moment in time captured forever, and remember this day, reflecting as he did on how much had changed since then, water flowing unstoppably towards the sea. Perhaps he would feel different then, or perhaps he wouldn't and this is how it would be from now on, until it was his turn to say goodbye.

Printed in Great Britain
by Amazon

15462543R00091